MW00893526

ALONE

By
Darrell Maloney

–1–

Dave couldn't get the tune out of his head. He'd heard it all morning long, off and on, playing quietly in the back of his skull. And it was driving him crazy.

Oh, it wasn't unpleasant. It was a happy little ditty. At least it sounded that way. It sounded more like sunshine and smiles, rather than rainclouds and foreboding.

Finally, he'd had enough.

"Okay, let's play a game," he announced while looking in the rearview mirror at Lindsey and Beth.

"I'll hum you a tune, and the first one to guess the tune gets a candy bar when we get to the airport."

Sarah looked at him from the passenger seat. With *that* look.

"Excuse me, mister? You're going to get the girls all hyped up on sugar just before I take them on a four hour plane ride?"

"Not both of them, honey. Just the one who guesses the name of the song."

"Uh… no. If that song is still bugging you, just hum it. If any one of us guesses it, you can buy each of us a cinnabon."

The girls laughed. Beth gave Lindsey a high five. Lindsey said, "All right! Go, Mom!"

Dave coughed. At first he had no words.

Then he found some, and stated the obvious.

"Why is it okay to get all three of you hyped up on sugar but not okay to do it to just one of you?"

"Because you know I have a thing for cinnabons. And I'm the mom. So that makes me the boss."

Lindsey broke out in uncontrollable laughter from the back seat, and Beth said, "Ooooohhh, Dad, you just got *owned.*"

"I don't know if it's worth it. I mean, those things aren't cheap, you know."

"Oh, we know, don't we girls?"

Two heads nodded up and down behind her.

"But, Dave, they are soooo worth the price. And I'll give you a bite. And think how sweet I'll taste when you kiss me goodbye."

Beth made a gagging sound.

"Besides, if you want us to help you with that song, you have to pay the piper. It's only fair. And if you don't, it'll continue to drive you crazy for days. Maybe even the whole week we're gone. And we'd feel so bad for you if that happened."

"Yeah, you're just oozing with sympathy for my plight."

Sarah smiled and blew him a kiss. She was even more gorgeous than the day they'd met thirteen years before. It suddenly dawned on him that he was an incredibly lucky man, to have such a beautiful wife and family. And that the price of three cinnabons wasn't that great, in the grand scheme of things.

In other words, he played right into Sarah's hands. She knew he would, as soon as she let the kiss fly.

"Okay, here goes."

Dave started humming the tune that had played in his mind a thousand times since the previous evening.

It took the three of them no more than ten notes. They'd have been "Name That Tune" champions in another era.

All three of them blurted out, almost simultaneously, "It's a Beautiful Day in the Neighborhood."

Then Dave felt incredibly stupid.

"Of course. How could I have not known that? The old Mr. Rogers theme song. Sheesh! Now I really feel dumb."

Sarah said, "Did you know that Fred Rogers was a Green Beret in Vietnam, and wore his red sweater to hide all of his tattoos?"

Dave scoffed.

"Where did you hear that?"

"On the internet. Why?"

"That story's been going around for years. It was debunked a long time ago. Mr. Rogers was a fine man, but he was never a Green Beret."

"Oh, yeah? Where did you hear that?"

"On the internet."

It was too much for Lindsey.

"Gee whiz, would you two stop believing what you read on the internet? Nearly all of it is garbage."

She turned to her little sister.

"Do we have to teach these old people *everything?*"

Beth said nothing but nodded her head decisively. She was in firm agreement.

Dave was a man of his word, and after the family checked in at the ticket kiosk and Sarah and the girls got their boarding passes, they made a beeline to Cinnabon.

"Daddy, are you going to walk us to the gate?"

"No, honey, I can't go through security without a boarding pass, so I'll walk you as far as I can and then you can give me a great big hug and a kiss."

"I wish you could come with us."

"I know, sugar. I wish I could too. But with two of the guys being sick at work, they just can't let me take vacation right now. Uncle Tommy will understand, and we can go fishing another time. And you'll be so busy helping Aunt Susan get everything ready for the wedding, you won't even have time to miss me."

"Bet I will!"

Sarah looked at him longingly. They were going to be apart for their twelfth anniversary. It would be the first one they'd missed.

It was as if he could read her mind.

"We'll do something special when you get back, I promise. We'll get a sitter and go spend the weekend at the lake. Just the two of us."

"I'd like that."

He walked the three special ladies in his life to the TSA checkpoint and got his hugs and kisses.

He held Sarah close and told her he loved her.

Little Beth rolled her eyes and said, "No mush, you two."

Dave paid her no mind. He looked Sarah in the eyes and said, "It'll seem like forever before I see you again."

Neither of them had a clue how true those words would be.

–2–

Dave was a builder by trade, but it was the off season, so he'd taken a second job to help pay the ever-growing expenses of feeding a family of four, and preparing for an uncertain future. They lived in a suburb on the northern outskirts of San Antonio. And even though San Antonio had moderate weather most of the year, it was cold enough in January and February to bring new house construction to a standstill.

However, cabinet building went on all year around.

Dave's second job was at a small cabinet shop. He made some of the cabinets he might later be installing in some of the new homes he built. In fact, the owner of the cabinet shop, Roger Hudson, had been a close friend for years. He made a point to buy Roger's cabinets whenever he could. They were well made and reasonably priced. And he was a big believer in buying local whenever he could.

Roger offered Dave the entire day to send his girls up north to Kansas City. It was the least he could do, he said. After all, they were short handed and in a pinch to complete a couple of contracts by deadline. And Dave had volunteered to stay behind and miss his sister in law's wedding to help out.

Dave said no thanks to the full day off. The girls weren't due to land in Kansas City until 6:10 p.m. due to a long layover at DFW. He could work the entire afternoon and still make it home in time for their phone call. He was looking forward to hearing all about the trip. It was six year old Beth's first time on an airplane, and she'd been talking about little else for weeks. Dave hoped she had a pleasant time, because he knew she'd go into great detail to tell him everything about it.

So working half a day was no big deal, really, and certainly no inconvenience. Dave liked this kind of work. He'd always been good with his hands, able to fashion pretty much anything out of anything else. Sarah joked that he was a lot like *MacGyver* from the old television series.

"If anyone could build a submarine out of a couple of paperclips, it's you."

He'd taken it as a compliment. But he was indeed one of those men who looked at a pile of junk and saw promise from it. So this job suited him very well.

The job also paid well, so it aided Dave and Sarah in another way that no one else knew about. Because they kept it a closely guarded secret.

Dave and Sarah were preppers. Had been for several years. They were convinced that something catastrophic was about to befall mankind, and would wipe out most of the world's population. And make it extremely difficult for the survivors to get by.

It started one night in 2010. They were sitting on the couch eating popcorn and flipping channels when they stumbled across a documentary about the Mayans. It piqued their curiosity, and they watched it to the end.

The narrator said that the Mayans predicted the end of the world on December 21, 2012. He didn't say how or why the Mayans made that prediction. But he did point out some astounding facts. Like, for example, that the Mayans had identified all the planets, and each of the planets' moons, without the aid of telescopes. After the program, Dave and Sarah had gone into their back yard and looked up at the sky. They couldn't tell the planets from the stars. All of them were just points of light. And they couldn't see any moons at all, save the earth's own.

Dave remembered Sarah saying, "How in the hell did they do that?"

The narrator had offered other information about the Mayans that was equally intriguing. They knew how to forecast earthquakes and tidal waves.

Dave had said, “That can’t be. Scientists today can’t even do that, and they have all kinds of fancy equipment.”

But the pair was curious enough to do their own research, and they found that most of what the narrator had said was true. The Mayans discovered the planets and their moons without telescopes. They did indeed leave behind schedules of coming tidal waves and earthquakes. And they did indeed make such predictions without the aid of any type of machinery.

The narrator was wrong about one thing, however. The Mayans never said the world was going to end on December 21, 2012.

What the Mayans actually said was that the “final period of progress” would begin on that date.

Scientists had been debating for a very long time exactly what the Mayans meant by “the last period of progress.”

Dave and Sarah wondered too. And that led to even more research. After hundreds of hours on line and at the local library, they believed that they’d finally discovered what the Mayans meant.

Another thing that intrigued scientists and archaeologists about the Mayans was their success in making other predictions. Predictions that had absolutely nothing to do with earthquakes and tidal waves.

Rather, these predictions pertained to things like automobiles, helicopters and machines.

The Mayans spoke of a time in the future when man would travel great distances on wheeled vehicles that would move under their own power. They would also fly, “like great winged birds in containers of metal” across the oceans to other lands of the world.

“Wait a minute,” Sarah had said with a shudder. The Mayans were a landlocked society. How did they know about oceans or tidal waves or airplanes? And how could they possibly know about other lands of the world? This is getting spooky."

The Mayans spoke of man building machines that would someday do most of his work for him. But they also cautioned that the survival of machines was subject to the whims of nature.

Dave and Sarah became convinced that the Mayans' "last period of progress" would mark the time that all the machines suddenly and permanently stopped working. And they believed it would happen as the result of nature.

"But what in the world could Mother Nature do that would knock out all the machines of the world? A hurricane or a tornado could certainly destroy a city, but it would have no affect on the machines in another country, or on another continent."

Sarah believed she found the answer when she was at the library one evening, looking through a picture book of the ancient Mayan temples. She noticed that many of their carvings portrayed the sun. So many, in fact, that she got the impression they worshipped it.

"Okay, just hear me out," she'd said when returning home that night.

"We know that they believed there would come a time when something would stop all the machines in the world, presumably all at the same time. And they said it would be a naturally occurring event of some type.

"But they never said it would originate on earth."

She smiled an accomplished smile, certain of her discovery.

"So, what are you saying? A meteorite or an asteroid hitting the earth? That would send a lot of dust and particulates into the atmosphere, and the earth would cool, possibly for many years. Most of the animals and plants would die. But how would that keep a gasoline engine from working?"

"No, honey. I said nothing about asteroids or meteorites. I think the threat is our own sun."

Dave scratched his head.

"Okay, I'm lost. I don't follow you at all."

She pulled out a book called *Electricity and the Cosmos*. On its cover was a rather magnificent photograph of a lightning filled sky setting a tree on fire.

"Still lost."

"Be patient, my love."

Sarah turned to a page she'd marked with a post-it note. And she read aloud to him.

"Electromagnetic pulses, or EMPs, are brief discharges of electricity which by themselves pose no health threat to man. However, they have the unfortunate effect of sending electrical current across positive and negative poles of batteries, across oppositely charged electronic components, across oppositely charged wires. The effective result is that anything an EMP touches is permanently shorted out."

She looked at him as his jaw dropped.

"Now you tell me, honey, what all modern machines have in common."

Dave thought for a moment and replied, "They all have batteries, or circuit cards, or some type of electronic components."

–3–

Sarah spent a whole week of her vacation time that year at the public library. The internet was a valuable source, but much of the reference material on the Mayans was not digitized. She felt almost like an antique as she pored over old fashioned hardback reference books and encyclopedias dating back to the 1950s.

Every evening, after the homework and chores were done and the girls were tucked safely in bed, the couple did more research on the internet.

In the end, they were convinced the earth was due a massive EMP, generated by a huge solar storm on the surface of the sun.

But when? The Mayans merely said the window opened for the event at the end of December, 2012. They didn't say how long the window would remain open.

The only clue they had was the Mayans' fascination with the number twelve. For some reason, the number was almost Biblical in Mayan seer and scientific circles. Most of their earthquake predictions went something like "On the one hundred and twentieth day after the twelfth day before the summer solstice." It seemed almost nonsensical, yet it obviously made great sense to the Mayans.

"What if they estimated the date of the EMP, and then counted back twelve months? That would mean the EMP would be December 21, 2013."

"Maybe. But then, they could just as easily have estimated the day and counted back twelve *years*. That would make it December 21, 2024."

In the end, they just didn't know.

But they did believe.

They believed the Mayans had proven themselves capable of many amazing things.

They believed that a primitive civilization that was familiar with the planets and their moons might also have a fascination with the sun.

They believed that a civilization intelligent enough to predict earthquakes with no modern equipment could do other things equally as amazing. Say, for example, have the ability to predict cyclical storms on the surface of the sun.

Lastly, they believed it was their duty to protect themselves and their family from the turmoil they were sure was coming.

It was on that day, in the spring of 2010, that they made the decision to be preppers.

Over the weeks that followed, they shared their findings with Sarah's brother and sister-in-law in Kansas City. They were cable television junkies and had already seen the prepper shows. It didn't take much to convince them to start prepping too.

They also discovered something the Mayans never mentioned. There was a way to protect some items from the effects of the EMP. It was called a Faraday cage, named after its inventor. The Faraday cage was basically a frame with a wire enclosure built around it. Items inside the cage were safe from electrical discharge even when electricity came into direct contact with the outside of the cage. The electricity didn't penetrate the cage. It simply encased the outside of the cage itself.

In 1961 a University of Texas student named Kit Foley discovered that the Faraday cage wasn't infallible. Metal items placed too close to the wire exterior of the cage could allow a small arc of electricity to fly across the space between the items and the outer skin of the cage.

Foley solved this problem by modifying the Faraday design, and lining it with foam rubber or with plywood. It was a more efficient, but costlier way to protect items from electrical surges. He called it a Foley cage.

Dave and Sarah knew how to protect the items they deemed essential.

And they had a plan in place to start prepping by stockpiling supplies that would help them survive after the EMP.

The only real obstacle they had left in their path was funding. Dave made a pretty good living in the construction trade, and Sarah made a pretty good salary as a fifth grade teacher. But in a troubled economy there just wasn't much left over for prepping.

So Dave started looking for a second job.

"It'll just be for a year, maybe a year and a half," Dave had said. "All the pay from the part time job will go to buying supplies and prepping materials. After we have everything we need, I'll quit."

They weren't counting on two things, though. First, prepping is an endless process. Every time Dave bought a new weapon or tool or generator, he saw something else he wanted. Like dried food, or night vision goggles, or a few cases of MREs.

The second thing they hadn't counted on was Dave falling in love with his part time job. He hit it off very well with the other workers. He had fun. It was more a hobby than a job, since he loved working with his hands.

At the end of the year and a half, he and Sarah sat down and discussed whether it would be a wise move for him to quit.

He still had a list of things he wanted to buy for their prepping mission.

Sarah said, "Well, I'll admit it hasn't affected your quality time with the girls. I mean, you gave up your softball and bowling leagues, so you're able to spend at least as much time with them as before you took the job.

"And as for me, I still get plenty of quality time with you. Even on the nights you work, you still make it to bed on time."

She giggled.

"And it darn sure hasn't affected our love life. Almost every night you work, you come home ravenous, anxious to make love to me."

She looked him square in the eye.

"And by the way, why is that, anyway?"

He shrugged his shoulders.

"I don't know. Maybe hanging around that small shop with all those guys for four hours makes me hunger for female company. Are you complaining?"

She purred like a kitten.

"Who, me? Oh, no, baby. Not at all."

So for a variety of reasons, Dave kept his part time job and continued to spend every dollar he earned there for prepping.

Right up until the day Sarah and the girls got on that airplane.

–4–

Dave checked his watch when he walked out of the cabinet shop. It was 4:35. He hadn't eaten anything since the cinnabon at the airport that morning, and he was famished.

He figured he had just enough time to stop by the Taco Cabana on his way home.

It was the closest he'd ever come to cheating on Sarah. His father had died prematurely, as had his grandfather. Both from heart attacks. Clogged arteries, his father's doctor had said.

He admonished Dave, "If you want to live longer than your father did, eat a low fat diet."

In most cases, Dave followed the doctor's advice. But there were certain things he just wasn't willing to give up.

Like barbacoa.

Barbacoa was slow roasted shredded beef. For hundreds of years, the vaqueros of old Mexico took the head of a cow and spit-roasted over a very low heat until the meat just peeled off the bone. They knew that the most tender and most flavorful of beef came from the cheeks and jowls.

And it made excellent tacos.

He stepped up to the counter at Taco Cabana and placed his order.

"I'd like two pounds of barbacoa to go, with refried beans and an extra dozen tortillas."

In the back of his head, he could almost hear Sarah admonishing him:

"David Wayne Speer Junior, what are you doing to yourself? You know that grease is going to go straight to your arteries!"

As the cashier handed him his change, he smiled in the knowledge that he'd be able to eat all the barbacoa tacos he wanted for at least the next four days. And as long as he got rid of the evidence, he'd get away with it. Sarah would never know.

For a brief second he felt guilty. He hated keeping secrets from his beloved Sarah. But, he reasoned, it could be worse. He didn't drink, like a lot of men did. He didn't do drugs either. Never had, not even as a kid. He didn't gamble or chase other women like some others did. Sarah was the most gorgeous woman he'd ever seen. He'd never seen another woman who could hold a candle to her. And even if he had, he wouldn't have strayed.

He enjoyed sports, but he wasn't one of those men who was addicted to sports and spent every waking moment in front of the television screen.

No, he decided. This was a relatively harmless vice, and really the only one he had. He might not be perfect, but all in all he was a pretty good husband.

After he got his order, he rewarded himself for being a pretty good husband by opening up the box and making himself a taco for the road.

Dave put the box of barbacoa and the trimmings onto the passenger seat of his Explorer and noticed that his right rear tire was low. He'd always had a bad habit of picking up nails on construction sites, so it didn't surprise him. In fact, he half expected it to happen regularly. Two days before he'd been scouting out a tract of land where he'd just signed a contract to build three single family homes in the summer.

It was a minor inconvenience, and no more. He knew the guys at the Zarzamora Tire Shop quite well, and they'd plug it for a six pack of Corona. He'd swing it by there on his way to the cabinet shop in the morning, he figured. And if it went flat before then, it was no big deal. He always carried a portable air compressor behind the driver's seat.

He checked his watch again as he drove down Royal Valley Drive. He was a block and a half from home. The girls should be landing any time now. In fact, if they had a tail wind, they may already have landed. And any minute now his cell phone would ring, and the girls would announce they were in Kansas City.

Little Beth would be all giggles and have stories to tell of their great adventure so far. And he couldn't wait to hear them.

And then the most curious thing happened.

His vehicle died.

–5–

He cursed aloud.

“Damn it!”

Things like this always seemed to happen at the worst possible time.

He checked his rearview mirror to make sure no one was behind him, since he was blocking the street. There was a car in the mirror, but it was a full block behind him.

That wasn’t a problem. He’d be long gone before it got to him.

Or so he thought.

He turned the key and got nothing but silence. No groan of a starter that told him the carburetor wasn’t getting any gas. No click click click of a loose terminal or a bad solenoid.

Nothing.

“Damn it!”

He pulled the hood release and got out of the Explorer. He bent over the engine expecting to find his battery cable had somehow popped completely off the battery. But he could find nothing amiss.

For a moment he stood there, scratching his head. Then he looked down the street at the car he’d seen in his rearview mirror and saw that it too had its hood up. The driver was doing the same thing Dave was: standing in front of his disabled car looking bewildered.

Dave got an uneasy feeling. He took his cell phone from his pocket. The screen was black and appeared to be off.

But it wasn’t off. It was shorted out. It would never work again.

“No! No! No!”

He cursed under his breath and started to sprint for home. He was sure he knew what was going on, but was praying it wasn’t so.

His neighbor two doors down tried to stop him as he ran by.

"Hey, Dave," he called out as he lifted the hood of his car. "Do you know anything about cars?"

Dave ignored him, not because he was a rude sort, but because he was a man on a mission.

He burst into his front door and tried the lights. None of them worked. The huge wall clock he and Sarah had bought together the month before no longer ticked.

Maybe it was just a coincidence, he tried to convince himself. Maybe it was a temporary power outage. Maybe a transformer blew out on a nearby power pole.

At exactly the same time several vehicles mysteriously died, and his cell phone turned into a worthless paperweight.

Maybe.

He desperately looked around for something electric that was working. Something. Anything.

He saw the MP-3 player that Sarah wore when she was on the treadmill every morning, doing her daily run. She always said she couldn't run without her music. He picked it up and turned it on. Nothing.

He ran to the kitchen and pulled open the drawer that held flashlights and spare batteries.

One by one, he turned on each of four flashlights.

None of them worked, even though he'd replaced the batteries just days before.

He went down to his knees and began to cry.

For more than an hour he sat there, on the kitchen floor, waiting for the kitchen phone to ring. He'd picked it up a dozen times, hoping to hear a dial tone and hearing nothing but silence.

He'd removed the battery in his cell phone an equal number of times, then replaced it. He seemed to remember an old saying about a fool doing the same thing over and over again, and expecting a different result.

But he had no choice. It was the only straw he had to grasp.

The only working thing he could find was the old fashioned wind up wrist watch he bought because the batteries kept wearing out on his old one. It ran off a spring that would keep good time, provided it was rewound at least every other day.

He found himself sitting in the kitchen, watching the shadows crawl higher and higher on the bare white walls as the setting sun dipped lower in the sky.

He was numb. He couldn't bear to think the thoughts that kept skirting the edges of his mind. Wouldn't think about them. He'd just take it for granted that yes, his family landed safely just before the power went out. In fact, they made good time and landed early. By the time the power outage blackened the Kansas City airport, they were surely on their way to Uncle Tommy's house.

No, that wasn't good enough. He couldn't bear to think they might be caught out in the open. Their flight made record time. Yes, that must be it. The flight made record time and arrived a full half hour ahead of schedule. They had time to get their luggage and drove to Uncle Tommy's house. They pulled up into the driveway just before the blackout, and they were safe and sound.

In fact, they were just ready to call him when everything died.

That's what happened. He was as sure of it as he was of anything else.

It had to be that way. Any other scenario was just too painful to consider.

On and off over the next few hours he got up and stretched his legs. He knew there was a lot of work to do. He just couldn't find the motivation to do it. So he got up periodically and stretched his legs, and walked around a bit.

During one such episode, he walked up the stairs. His subdivision sat upon a hill, and in the distance on a clear night, he could actually see downtown San Antonio. On those nights, the Hemisfair Tower shone like a beacon in the distance, some nine miles away.

It occurred to him, while sitting on the kitchen floor, that perhaps the blackout wasn't a widespread thing after all. That maybe, just maybe, the power lines shorted out in his area alone. Maybe some freakish weather conditions caused the shorted power lines to short out other electronics in close proximity.

Maybe the rest of the world was okay, outside his neighborhood.

Maybe his wife and daughters had been trying to call him for hours. Maybe *they* were worried about *him,* and wondering why he wouldn't answer either phone.

Maybe.

But not likely.

With much anticipation, he'd climbed the stairs, praying that he'd look out that south window and see the downtown skyline aglow in the distance. And then he could walk toward the lights until he found a convenience store or a grocer that had power. Then he'd use a pay phone to call his wife and tell her he was okay.

Only the skyline wasn't lit up in the distance. The night was crystal clear. He could see twinkling stars in every corner of the sky, and knew it wasn't clouds that were blocking the city lights.

There were no city lights.

And he stumbled back to the kitchen, where he curled into a ball and cried.

Sometime later he finally began to regain his wits. Regardless of what did or didn't happen to his family, he had things to do. And perhaps the way to keep from going insane was to stay focused on the tasks at hand. To keep busy. To keep his mind occupied.

He looked at the face of his wind up watch, the luminescent hands glowing in the dark and telling him it was almost three a.m.

He'd have to hurry. The sun would come up around six thirty or so, and he needed to finish his mission and be back in the house before then.

He went through the first floor of the house, opening all of the window curtains. He'd use the full moon and cloudless sky to his advantage. There wasn't much light out there, but he'd let as much of it in as he could. He'd still be stumbling around in the darkness, but it wouldn't be quite pitch black.

Almost, but not quite.

–6–

Dave found his keys where'd he'd last remembered seeing them. In his panic to get home, he'd left them hanging in the knob on the front door. He kicked himself. If the looters had been out and about, they'd have just walked right in, before he was set up to defend himself.

From his front porch he sniffed the air. He didn't smell any smoke. He heard absolutely nothing. He surmised that the residents for the most part probably considered this just a freak power outage. They probably assumed that the lights would come back on at any moment.

He suspected, and indeed hoped, that the looting and riots wouldn't start until the next night, as it started to become apparent to people that this was more than a temporary situation.

And as more and more people started to panic.

He walked back into his house and locked the front door. Then he made his way into his garage and felt his way around until he found a red plastic handle hanging on the end of a short white cord from his electric garage door opener.

The emergency release. He pulled it, and the garage door popped as it disengaged itself from the motor.

Dave carefully opened the noisy door by hand, raising it slowly and cursing under his breath with every squeak and groan it made.

He didn't know if his neighbors could see what he was doing, or even if they were watching, but he had no choice. This could only be done under cover of darkness, and the second night would be too dangerous. He only hoped he hadn't waited too long.

He hopped in Sarah's Honda Accord and inserted the key to unlock the gear shift. Then he put it into neutral and slowly pushed it down the driveway and into the street.

Then he pushed it forward, three houses down the street, and parked it in front of the Smith house.

The Smiths were on a week long trip to Disney World in Orlando, and would surely never be back. Hopefully a car parked in front of their house would keep the looters away for a few days, until Dave had a chance to go over himself and empty the house of anything he could use.

To help his cause, He came back ten minutes later and hung a note on their front door. The note, which he'd scrawled on a sheet of white copy paper with a black marker, was barely legible in the moonlight.

It said:

HEAVILY ARMED AND PISSED OFF
IF YOU BREAK IN HERE, YOU DIE.

There was still much to do. When he came back to the Smith home the second time, he brought a Phillips screwdriver and four five gallon Jerry cans from a high shelf in his garage.

He carried the cans to the back of Sarah's Honda and crawled underneath her gas tank. There, in a neat row, he punctured the bottom of the tank four times by holding the point against the tank and then hitting the screwdriver with the heel of his hand.

Four streams of gasoline immediately started streaming from the tank, and he positioned the Jerry cans underneath the streams to catch it. He didn't have a clue how much gas she had in the tank, since the gauge wasn't working without battery power. But he hoped she had twenty gallons worth.

If she didn't, there were plenty of other vehicles on the street.

While the cans were filling, he went back to his garage and collected a pile of old newspapers from the same shelf he'd taken the Jerry cans from. The newspapers had been on the shelf for months. They were yellow and had started to curl on the edges.

He tossed them onto the front porch. Then he took three lawn chairs and two loungers from the patio in front of his house and threw them unceremoniously into the back yard. In another time, he enjoyed sitting on the chairs, sipping iced tea with Sarah and the girls, while waving at the neighbors and watching the world go by.

Now, he suspected, those times were gone forever.

He walked back to the Honda to check on the progress of the Jerry cans. They were only half full. Obviously filling a five gallon can with a stream of gas no wider than a screwdriver tip was a slow process.

He went back to the house and stumbled around in the darkness until he made his way to his office, then removed a file from the very back of the bottom drawer of his filing cabinet.

In the same drawer was something else he'd need. Several decorative scented candles. The scent didn't matter to him. He couldn't have cared less what they smelled like, as long as they gave him the light he needed to finish this part of his plan.

Back to the kitchen he went, lighting the candle on the kitchen counter with a box of long kitchen matches in the back of the silverware drawer.

He opened the folder and took out three copies of a fill-in-the blank foreclosure notice. He'd downloaded it off the internet several months before.

All three copies were already filled in, with their home address and a fictitious bank. They were signed by an equally bogus "loan officer," someone named Jack Green, on the bottom right corner of each document.

All that was left to do was fill in the date block at the top of each form. Then he took a roll of clear packing tape and taped one copy on the garage door, one on the front door, and one on the inside of the picture window in the front room.

His goal was for any looters who came around to see the foreclosure notices and think the house was vacant. Vacant houses contain no food or other pilferable items. Hopefully the looters would move on to another house and loot it instead.

The lack of cars in the driveway and lack of lawn furniture on the front patio would, he hoped, provide further proof that the house was unoccupied.

So would the yellowed newspapers on the doorstep.

After hanging the signs, he walked back down to the Honda to find the Jerry cans full and overflowing. He was spilling gasoline on the street, but it was unavoidable. And in the grand scheme of things, it was the last thing he needed to worry about. The tank only held twenty something gallons. He'd just taken twenty of it. There couldn't be too much left.

But he figured twenty gallons would fuel his generator for quite awhile.

It took him two trips to get the Jerry cans back into his garage. Then he closed the garage door and locked it.

There were still a thousand and one other things that needed to be done. But every one of them was infinitely more difficult to do in the dark. And he finally felt tired enough to grab a little sleep.

He looked at his watch. It was 4:45 a.m.

He blew out the candle, went upstairs to his bedroom, and laid down on his bed.

–7–

Dave awoke to voices. For a brief moment he imagined they were the voices of his daughters. But no. These were men's voices, and they weren't familiar.

Then he remembered the dire situation he was in, and jumped out of bed.

He made his way to the bedroom window and carefully lifted the edge of one blind. In the street, directly in front of his house, were three of his neighbors,

Dave couldn't make out what they were saying, but he did catch an occasional phrase.

"Damn power company."

"Wife is afraid."

"Need to call a tow truck."

He was tempted for a moment to go out and join them, just for the comfort that other human beings could offer. Dave had always been a social kind of guy, had always enjoyed the company of others, and he didn't like being alone.

It wasn't supposed to be like this. He and Sarah knew the blackout was coming, eventually. But the plan was for them to have each other. He didn't like that he was going into this adventure alone.

In the end, he held firm. Sarah wasn't with him, but he'd carry on with their game plan as though she were.

And their game plan from the beginning was to keep a very low profile, and to try to convince looters and thieves that their house was vacant, so they'd bypass it and go elsewhere.

They were so convinced that the EMP was coming that they purposely grew apart from their neighbors. They only knew a couple of them by name. And none of them were so close that they would be surprised to see that the Speer house was suddenly vacant.

But he still had a long way to go to complete the charade.

As he watched his neighbors disperse and go back into their houses, he thought through the long list of things he had to do. There was a lot for one man to handle alone. But that wasn't necessarily a bad thing. He knew the busier he was, the less time he'd have to think about Sarah and the girls. And to wonder…

Dave figured he had two things he had to do first. While he was at the window, he looked over the house across the street and could see the water tower to the north. He hadn't tried the faucet yet, but he was certain the machinery at the water plant was out. Unless their pumps were protected from electrical surges like EMPs, they wouldn't be able to pump fresh water to the city.

Or to make more drinking water once their supply was exhausted.

That meant the only water available would be gravity fed, for those residents who were lucky enough to live close enough to a water tower.

Like he was.

And he had to scramble quickly.

He suspected that there were still a lot of people who hadn't yet figured out that this wasn't a typical blackout. And those same people were probably flushing their toilets and taking showers. Some fools were probably watering their lawns.

He needed to get as much of the available water as he could. Before it was gone.

He rushed to the kitchen and turned on the faucet. It wasn't as strong as its usual flow, but at least it was flowing. He scrambled upstairs and pulled down the fold-up ladder that led to the attic.

Up in the attic, he started throwing down black garbage bags. One by one, until he had a pile of about twenty bags.

Each plastic bag contained empty two liter soda bottles. The family had been collecting them for over two years.

It was Sarah's idea.

"We'll need a method to capture rain water once we can't get water from the city any more. Instead of drinking the soda and taking the bottles to the recycling center, let's rinse them out, collapse them so they take up less space, and then put the caps back on them so they don't expand again. Then we can put them in trash bags and store them in the attic until we need them."

Dave was a bit hesitant at first, until it dawned on him that the empty soda bottles would make an excellent second layer of insulation for their attic.

After all, the empty bottle was everything good insulation should be. It trapped air, was light as a feather, and could easily be distributed on top of the existing attic installation. Over the course of the two years, he figured they'd collected at least four or five hundred. The plan was to fill as many as possible every time it rained, then purify it as needed to get through to the next rainfall.

He got back to the kitchen and ripped open the first bag, then filled twenty bottles or so, before it dawned on him there was a better way. Since the water was running at a reduced rate, it took a full two or three minutes to fill each one.

He could be doing other things instead of standing in front of the sink.

He went to the upstairs bathroom, took a clean towel from the linen closet, and wiped the tub. The tub was sparkling clean anyway, because Sarah was a clean freak. But he'd feel better about drinking the water later on if he knew in his own mind that he'd wiped the tub.

He plugged the drain and turned the water on, then left the tub to fill.

Then he went downstairs to do the same thing to the other bathroom.

He figured it would take the tubs at least an hour to fill at the reduced flow rate, so he'd keep an eye on them and get his other project done.

Dave's other pressing project was to clear out the front bedroom, so he could raise the blinds and complete the illusion that the house was vacant. Just in case anyone peeked in the window, he wanted them to see a vacant house and nothing more.

For the next three hours, Dave moved every single thing from the front room to the garage, starting with the furniture. Then he took down the curtains, and removed everything from the walls.

When everything was out of the room, he stood at the window and looked over his efforts. He saw three doors in a line on the interior wall. One led to the downstairs bathroom. He left that one open, and removed everything from the bathroom that might indicate someone lived there.

The second door led to the hallway. He left that door completely closed, and hoped that looters would assume it was a closet.

The real closet door, on the other hand, would be left just a little bit open. Any looters looking in the window would assume it led into the rest of the house, but wouldn't be able to see far enough into it to realize it was only a closet.

The illusion was complete.

When he was finished he lifted a blind to make sure no one was in his yard, then raised the blinds all the way to the top.

Just as they'd be if the house were really empty.

-8-

As the sun set low in the sky on the second day after the blackout, Dave was getting lonely and desperate to talk to someone.

And he couldn't get his mind off of Sarah and the girls. He had to do something to keep from going insane, so he took a green hardbound logbook from his desk drawer and started writing.

I don't even know why I'm writing this. To keep myself from going crazy, I suppose.

No, that's only partially true. I'm writing it partially to keep from going crazy, and partially because I'm hoping that talking to you will ease my pain.

I love you, Sarah, with all my heart. All I ever wanted to do was make you happy, from the first moment I ever laid eyes on you so many years ago. I don't think I ever told you that I loved you from the beginning. I saw you from across the bar and I was struck like a bolt of lightning. I was hooked from that very first moment and there was no going back. You thought it was a pure accident that I dropped my keys as you walked by.

But it was no accident. I dropped them on purpose. I was in love with you even then. And I saw you walking out the door with your friends. Walking out of my life. And I had to do something. So I dropped my keys to stop you, and then struck up a conversation. And the rest, as they say, is history.

I don't know what's going to happen to me in the weeks or months ahead. Hell, I don't even know if you and my angels are still alive. But I never told you that story before. For some reason I thought you needed to know.

It's been two full days since the power went out. I've made the house appear vacant. I think it helped. Last night, the second night, the chaos started. I counted twelve gunshots through the night. Some of them sounded like they were on our street.

I peeked out of an upstairs window, the one in Beth's room, and saw a lot of shadowy figures out and about. I even saw two men with a torch. They came to our door, and read the foreclosure sign. Then they left again.

I'm trying to stay upbeat. I'm trying to believe that most of the people I saw were merely out looking for food or water for their families.

But then I wonder why they're using the cover of darkness. And I think that if they weren't up to no good, they'd be searching for food and water during the daytime.

I suspect that there's a lot of ugliness out there. And I think it'll get a lot worse before it gets better.

The only way I can survive this ordeal is by thinking that you landed safely, and are with Tommy and Susan, safe and sound. And that some day, somehow, we'll be together again.

I was able to fill almost three hundred bottles of water before the taps ran dry. I expected there to be much more water in the tower on Pine Street, but I guess others had the same idea and stocked up as well.

I'm not worried. This will be plenty to last until the next rainfall, and I'll have the catch systems up and running by then. Plus, we've got the twenty cases of drinking water, so I won't even have to break into the tap water for awhile.

Storing the empty soda bottles in the attic was the best idea you ever had. Well, maybe the second best idea, after marrying me. In any event, water shouldn't be a problem for the foreseeable future. Thank you for that.

I'm out of daylight. I've decided to save the candles for the wintertime, so I can use them for heat as well as light. That means working from dawn to dusk, then crashing during the nighttime hours. That's okay, though, because I'm exhausted.

Good night, Doll. Kiss the girls for me.

–9–

Dave awoke to the birds singing from the Sycamore tree outside his bedroom window. The sun was already up and well above the horizon. He'd lost at least an hour of daylight, but he didn't see it as a major problem. He was exhausted from the day before, and needed the rest.

He had two items on his agenda today. First, he'd finish up the project he'd started the day before, and when he was finished his perimeter fence would be fortified as an added measure against prowlers.

After he was done with that, he'd break into his Faraday cage and take out his generator. Then he'd use some of the pre-drilled plywood and two by fours from the lumber pile in the garage and build a small soundproof enclosure for it.

Once the enclosure was done, he'd be able to run his generator for short periods of time in his garage without his neighbors being able to hear it.

If he happened to finish both of the projects today, he'd move onto a third: putting together his outhouse. But there was no real hurry on that. The hole he'd dug in the back corner of the yard would suffice for now.

He debated with himself about the pace he wanted to set for himself. He knew that there were a hundred different things to do before he could live a reasonably comfortable existence.

His initial impulse was to work his ass off and get everything done as quickly as he could.

But the other side of the coin was, once everything was done his biggest enemy would be boredom. Once he finished all his projects, there would be little to do. And he wasn't the type of person who could stand still for very long.

In the end he wound up in something of a compromise with himself. Every day, he'd select a couple of projects to do, based on their order of importance. If he finished those projects, he'd take the rest of the day off and read, or listen to the music on the small boom box in the Faraday cage.

If he didn't finish, he'd work right up until sundown, and then crash for the night.

The previous day, he'd been working his way around the perimeter of his privacy fence, installing screws into holes that he'd pre-drilled months before.

His fence was typical of all the others in the neighborhood. Fence posts were planted on eight foot centers, and three two-by-four stringers were run horizontally between the posts. Pine pickets, six feet tall and six inches wide, were nailed to the stringers to complete the fence.

Months before, Dave had spent the better part of a week with a rechargeable drill, going from one picket to the next, and drilling two holes into each picket, an inch from the top of the fence.

Sarah thought he had lost his mind and went out to see what he was doing.

She said, "Hey, honey, are you okay?"

"Sure. Why do you ask?"

"Well, I've been watching you work your way down the fence for the last half hour. You're drilling hundreds of holes, but not doing anything with them. It just seems kind of strange to me, that's all. Should I call a shrink?"

"No, smartass. I'm pre-drilling holes so when the world goes black we can fortify our fence."

"Oh, yes! That's right, I forgot. And how, exactly, is a bunch of holes going to fortify our fence?"

"Because in the garage is a forty pound box of two inch screws that we'll screw into the holes, facing the outside, when the stuff hits the fan. Anybody who tries to climb over the fence will shred his hands to pieces, and I'm guessing he'll go to another yard that's easier to get into."

"But I thought we were going to hide in plain sight, by making the house appear to be vacant."

"We are. This is just an added precaution, in case somebody is too stupid to get the message."

"Smart. I guess you never can be too careful, huh?"

"That's my thinking. This will take a little time, but it's a really cheap security system. Just some cheap screws and some time is all."

"So, you're going all the way around the yard?"

"Yep. And not only our yard, but the Hansen house as well."

The Hansen house was a large two story structure directly behind them. They shared a common back fence.

The Hansens had moved out more than a year before, when their walls started developing severe cracks. An insurance inspector pulled up the carpet and padding, and discovered that the walls weren't the only thing cracking. So was the foundation.

The city condemned the structure as unsafe. The insurance company accused the builder of improperly packing the soil before the slab was poured.

The builder, in turn, said there must have been an earthquake. He denied responsibility for what he called an "isolated act of nature."

The case had been tied up in the courts for months. Dave and Sarah were hoping it took years to resolve. The house was huge, and would provide enough lumber to provide their firewood needs for at least a couple of years. Also, the back yard was three times the size of their own, with an eight foot privacy fence. It would be perfect for growing crops.

But possibly the best things were the apple and pecan trees in the front of the back yard, close to the house. They were five years old now with established root systems. That meant they'd survive on their own, with only minimal watering needed during an occasional drought.

"Aren't you afraid that someone will see you over there, drilling holes in their fence?"

"Who's coming? The Hansens have already moved up to Waco. The bank never comes around anymore. They've turned it all over to the lawyers."

Sure enough, Dave was able to spend three days in the back yard of the Hansen house, drilling two small holes in each of the six hundred eighty four fence slats.

And no one had a clue.

He was finding now, though, that drilling hundreds of holes was a piece of cake, when compared with screwing in hundreds of screws without the aid of an electric drill.

Oh, he did have a drill in his Faraday cage. And he had a generator to power it. Or, at least to charge the batteries which would power it.

The problem was, he couldn't try his hardest to convince the neighbors and passersby that the house was vacant, and then be working in the back yard with a noisy drill.

So here he was, with an orange and white Home Depot pocket apron around his waist, right over the top of his military surplus web belt and holster. Both pockets on the apron were full of two-inch long black screws, and he was slowly moving from picket to picket screwing the screws into the holes.

It was a slow process, and a painful one. His forearms were on fire and he frequently had to stop and rest, when his hands temporarily ceased to function. He was convinced that by the time he finished the task, his forearms would be as big as a bodybuilder's, and would be so heavy he wouldn't be able to lift them.

At a little after three p.m., he was sick of screwing screws into fence pickets.

He figured that what he needed more than anything was a change of scenery.

So he took a break, just long enough to eat four barbacoa tacos. He'd retrieved the food from his Explorer the first night of the blackout, while his Jerry cans were filling underneath Sarah's Honda. Initially, he'd kept it in the refrigerator, hoping it didn't spoil before he finished eating it all.

Once the refrigerator was no longer cool on the inside, he moved the barbacoa to the chest freezer in the garage. The stuff in the freezer had started to thaw after two days, but was still cold enough to keep his barbacoa from spoiling. At least until he could polish it off.

Once he finished eating, he went into the garage to start his second project.

Like many people, Dave and Sarah only parked one of their cars in their two car garage. Usually, people who did that made the second half of their garage into a workshop, or a storage area.

And technically, Dave and Sarah did that too. But the stuff in their storage area looked anything but typical. For on the unused half of their garage was a huge pile of lumber and plywood.

The bottom layer of the stack consisted of four sheets of half inch plywood, laid side by side. There were nineteen other similar layers, for a total of eighty uncut sheets of plywood. After that were two layers of two by fours and four by four fence posts, followed by several pieces of plywood that had been cut into various shapes and sizes. The cut pieces all had holes drilled into them in random places, as did many of the two by fours. On top of all of that, from the top of the stack and stretching almost to the ceiling, was Dave's Faraday cage.

Boxes of survival supplies and dried food were stacked all around the pile.

They'd tried to plan for everything. And everything meant not only wood for a soundproof enclosure for the generator. It also meant wood for a safe room and an outhouse.

The cut pieces of plywood and lumber also had vague markings on them in black sharpie, that seemingly made no sense at all.

But Dave knew what they meant.

Dave knew because all of the pieces with holes and markings had been prefabricated. Cut for specific reasons. They'd all been assembled to make sure they fit together properly, and then taken apart again.

Dave took a propane lantern and screwed it onto a small disposable bottle of propane. He lit it and placed it on the floor next to the lumber pile. So he wouldn't be overcome by carbon dioxide, he left the door to the house open and opened the patio door on the other side of the kitchen. He hoped it would provide enough ventilation.

Then he got to work.

–10–

Dave worked fast. He knew the dangers of carbon dioxide poisoning. He knew it crept up on its unsuspecting victims, made them think everything was fine until they passed out. And that sometimes they never woke up.

He took a pair of wire cutters off a pegboard on the wall where he kept most of his tools. He snipped the heavy chicken wire that covered all six sides of his Faraday cage, and removed one of the panels.

Then he grabbed several appliances from it. The three thousand watt generator. A battery charging station. A small television set and DVD player. A coffee pot and microwave.

And finally, in the back of the cage, he found what he was looking for. A large cardboard box marked "flashlights, floodlights and batteries."

"All right!" he said. "Come to Daddy, so we can get you hooked up. It's starting to get stuffy in here."

Dave opened the box and took out a large camping light. Made to light a large tent, it worked equally well to light a large room. And it worked on six "D" batteries.

Most of the batteries in the box were rechargeable. But there were also some old fashioned disposable batteries that were fully charged and ready to go. Those were the ones he put into the camp light.

Once the batteries were in, he held his breath and turned on the switch. The light came on instantly, and he breathed a sigh of relief.

The Faraday cage had worked as advertised. Everything inside it had been saved from the EMP.

He turned off the propane lantern and unscrewed it from the small propane bottle. He put the bottle back where he'd gotten it, in the corner of the garage with four twelve pack cases of similar bottles. From now on, the propane would be used solely for boiling his drinking water.

The camp light gave him plenty of light to finish up his project: selecting the pieces for his soundproof generator box.

Each piece was marked in sharpie, with the letter "G". It was followed by more cryptic code that only Dave and Sarah understood.

For example, "G-L-O" meant the piece belonged to the generator box, was the left wall, and that the markings were written on the outside.

It wasn't unlike a big tinker toy set. All of the pieces had already been assembled once. But for the box to go back together exactly the same way, all of the pieces had to be returned to their exact original position. Otherwise the screw holes wouldn't line up.

The generator box only had five sides. Without an adequate air supply, it would cut out and die. Therefore, the front of it, or the side facing the door leading into the house, was left off the structure.

The structure was for soundproofing only. It was never intended to protect the occupants of the house from carbon dioxide poisoning. It was only meant to muffle the sound of the generator so it wouldn't attract undue attention from passersby or looters.

It took Dave almost until sundown to find the pieces of two by fours that made up the structure's frame, and to screw everything into place. Then he positioned the generator within the enclosure, and stood back to inspect his handiwork.

So far, so good. But he wasn't finished yet. Behind the pile of lumber, up against the wall, next to several heavy plastic tarps, he retrieved two rolls of sound insulation and wrapped the entire structure.

Then he stepped back again to admire his work.

It wasn't pretty. But then, it wasn't meant to be. It was meant to be effective, and he had confidence it would be. The generator ran quietly anyway, no louder than a car idling. Inside the structure, the sound would be muffled even further. The first time he'd assembled it, the previous summer, he stood in his driveway on a still night, with the garage door open. He couldn't hear the generator running at all. With the door closed, he was confident he could run it safely for short periods without anyone on the outside knowing.

He went back to his fence project. It was twilight now, but he could already see a half moon in the sky. There was no need to stop working. Not just yet.

He'd already found that it was good to exhaust himself before going to bed. That way he'd fall asleep almost immediately, instead of thinking about Sarah and the girls.

And wondering if they were dead or alive.

So for another two hours, until just past eleven, he inserted screws into the fence.

By the time he'd finally done the last of them, his arms felt like putty and burned.

But anybody dumb enough to climb over this fence, by God, would pay a very heavy price.

-11-

I'm writing this by candlelight. It's about three in the morning, and I'm having trouble sleeping. I pray every night that you made it safely to Kansas City and met Tommy and Susan there. I know they're taking good care of you, if only you were able to make it that far.

As for the other option, that your plane fell from the sky, I'm trying not to think of that. It keeps popping into my head, and I try to force it back out again. It's just an option I refuse to accept.

It occurred to me that I haven't cried for you yet. I wondered why. And then I realized that crying for you would be tantamount to admitting that you didn't make it. And I will never admit that.

As for me, I'll continue to press on. If I knew you were all dead, I'd end my own life in a heartbeat. But I believe you're still alive. I have to.

I believe something else, too. I believe that someday, somehow, we'll be together again. I will find you, and I will find a way to get you back here. I promise you that.

I'm just not ready to give you all up yet.

The fence project is finished in our yard as well as the Hansen house. I've also vacated the front room and cleared out the driveway. It appears to have worked. I've seen people reading the foreclosure signs and then leaving, without breaking in or knocking on the door. I don't know if they were bad men looking to loot our belongings, or just desperate men begging for food or water. In the end, it doesn't matter. I've got plenty of both, but won't be sharing it. That may not be the Godly thing to do, but I'm not giving it all away to strangers and then running short when you guys get back here. So I'll continue to conserve it as best I can, and to make it last as long as possible.

I can hear gunshots in the distance. Even more than last night. I fear the world is turning into an ugly place. I only pray that you are safe.

I've decided to let the rabbits out of their cages tomorrow. I'm also going to assemble the outhouse. I'm tired of pissing into a hole in the ground.

Well, I guess that even with the outhouse I'll still be doing that. But at least I'll have some privacy.

Good night, sweet Sarah. I love you.

–12–

Dave awoke at mid morning, and looked at his watch. He'd forgotten to wind it the day before. For a brief moment he panicked, then decided to reset it for twelve when the sun was at its highest point and call that good enough.

He cursed himself for wasting so much of the day when there was still so much to be done.

First, he went to the window, and carefully lifted one of the blinds to look down at the street below. There wasn't anyone out and about. Perhaps the distant gunshots were keeping everyone in their houses. Still, he expected to see more people looking for food and water.

In the street, he could see a box of corn flakes and two cans of V-8 juice, still attached to their plastic carrier. He wondered where they came from. Dropped by a looter in the darkness, perhaps?

Then he saw a front door open, at the house across the street and two houses over.

Someone else had also seen the corn flakes and V-8. Someone perhaps a bit more desperate than Dave.

Dave watched as the man, who he recognized but never met, scurried out to the street and grabbed the items. Then he ran back into his house and closed the door.

Dave wondered how desperate his neighbors would become a week from now. Or two weeks, when their pantries were running low.

Then he heard gunshots again. These were much closer than the ones the night before. They sounded like they came from the end of his own block. Three gunshots, a few seconds apart. Then a fourth shot, maybe thirty seconds later.

He picked up the AR-15 he kept leaning against the window sill. He didn't expect any trouble. After all, who would assault an empty house?

But somehow just holding the weapon, and knowing he was ready to use it, gave him some comfort.

His second AR-15 was downstairs, by the back door. When he worked outside, he kept it within a few yards at all times.

Just in case.

Another twenty minutes ticked by before Dave decided he was wasting his time, standing by the window. There was no assault coming. Maybe another day, but not today.

He wondered about the gunshots. In all likelihood, he'd never know what they were all about. He and Sarah had discussed many times what the world would be like in the weeks and months following the blackout. They knew that as the situation became more and more desperate, that the weak would decide to take the easy way out.

Was that what he'd heard? A father, killing his family, then turning the gun on himself? He expected a lot of that to happen, but not quite so soon. Maybe it was a homeowner, scaring away looters. He was sure it wasn't a firefight. He heard only one weapon, he was sure of it.

Then he put it out of mind, confident that whatever it was, it was no threat to him. He expected to hear a lot more gunshots in the weeks ahead. This was surely just the beginning. And he had better things to worry about.

He was famished, and it occurred to him that he hadn't eaten since noon the previous day. The barbacoa was all gone now, and he'd have to start looking for something else to eat.

He went to the refrigerator and opened it. It was still cool, but not cool enough to keep anything fresh.

He took the top off the milk and sniffed it. It was sour.

"Damn!"

He kicked himself. He should have drank the milk before it went bad. At this point, he couldn't afford to waste any food. He needed to be smarter in the future.

He took a package of bologna from the meat tray and a loaf of bread from the pantry, and made himself three sandwiches. He wasn't crazy about bologna, but that no longer mattered. It was no longer food. It was merely fuel, something to keep his body running, and it no longer mattered if he liked it or not. Nothing could go to waste.

Not anymore.

He lathered the sandwiches with mayonnaise. He despised mayonnaise. Always had. But he was shifting from a mindset of eating what he liked to considering food as essential calories. Nothing more, nothing less.

In order to keep up his strength, he knew he had to take in two thousand calories a day. It didn't really matter that much what form those calories took.

The mayonnaise was very high in calories, and would only last a few more days without refrigeration. Once it went bad, the calories it contained were wasted.

And that was just unacceptable.

Luckily, the temperatures were still cool. It was the transition time between winter and spring. Nights were still a bit chilly, and daytime temperatures were still mostly cool. That would help the perishables keep a little bit longer.

He went through the refrigerator to survey what was left. He'd use as much as he could, even if it meant eating the rest of the mayonnaise right out of the jar. He wouldn't waste calories if he could avoid it, no matter how disgusting it was.

He couldn't help but smile. He'd always had a friendly debate with Sarah about the whole Miracle Whip versus mayonnaise thing. It was his contention that there were only two types of people in the world.

Those who loved mayonnaise and those who loved Miracle Whip.

He believed that those who grew up in a Miracle Whip house, as he did, loved the stuff and hated mayo. Those who grew up on mayo, as Sarah did, hated Miracle Whip.

Early in their relationship, they decided to compromise, and keep both. They'd let their children decide for themselves which one they liked.

And to their credit, Lindsey and Beth both sided with their dad and said Miracle Whip was the best.

But Sarah took it well, proclaiming, "Good! That just leaves more of the *good stuff* for me."

Dave felt his eyes moisten from the memory of his girls, and shook his head in an effort to chase away the thought.

Maybe later on he'd have time for sorrow. Now he wouldn't allow himself the luxury. He wouldn't be one of the weak who blew their own brains out because they couldn't cope with the heartache and the stress.

Not him. No way.

After Dave finished his sandwiches, he took the meat from the refrigerator and carried it to the chest freezer in the garage. He was confident that the well-insulated freezer would keep his perishable food relatively fresh until he could eat it all.

Once done, he went back to his pile of lumber and pulled out all of the pieces marked with an "O."

"O" stood for "outhouse."

Like the generator structure, he'd already built the outhouse once. The summer before he'd assembled it in the corner of the back yard, well away from the house. He'd called Sarah out to show it off, and she'd turned up her nose and said, "Seriously? You want me to use that?"

But she was joking. She was holding out hope that the Mayans were wrong about the solar storms and the

EMPs that would be coming their way. But she also knew that if it did happen, there would be drastic changes in their lives. And in a newly chaotic world this would be a relatively minor adjustment.

The one thing she asked for was a padded toilet seat, and he gave in to that. It was the least he could do.

He'd been using a hole he'd dug up against the fence, and was looking forward to something a bit more comfortable. So this was one of his two projects for the day.

The other was to set the rabbits loose.

–13–

Dave found all of the pieces to his outhouse and carried them into the back yard. Then he went back for a coffee can full of hardware marked "Outhouse." Lastly, he took the two screwdrivers he'd been using on the fence project the night before and two bottles of water, and placed them on the covered deck in his back yard.

He stood in the doorway between the pantry and the garage, looking around to make sure he had everything he needed.

Once he fired up the generator, it would be several hours before he could safely go into the garage again. So it was important that he not forget something.

Satisfied he hadn't left any pieces or tools behind, he went to one of his Jerry cans and took a glass measuring cup from one of the shelves.

He measured out one cup of gasoline and poured it into the generator's fuel tank. Then he primed it four times and pulled the crank to start it up.

The generator came to life.

After he bought the generator the previous year, he experimented with it to see how long it would run on a cup of gasoline. His tests varied, from just over an hour to almost two hours. Averaged out, it was right at an hour and a half.

It had occurred to Dave a couple of nights before, when he was laying in bed after being awakened by distant gunshots, that the chest freezer might still work. There were few electronic parts in it to short out. When he'd examined it, he discovered that the power cord was melted, but the compressor showed no signs of wear.

He took an old extension cord from the garage and replaced the cord, then crossed his fingers.

If it did work, it would enable him to freeze excess fruits and vegetables from his garden for use during the winter months. The generator was large enough to power the chest freezer in the garage, as well as several other small electrical items within the house.

He moved the freezer away from the wall, hoping beyond hope that the condenser was running. When he saw that it was he muttered, "Hallelujah!"

It was a small victory, sure. But he'd take them whenever he could get them.

He walked into the house, making sure that the door closed securely behind him. He wouldn't go back into the garage for several hours. That would give the deadly carbon monoxide time to seep out of the cracks around the overhead doors after the generator ran out of fuel and died.

In the pantry, an extension cord came under the door. The hundred foot cord ran through the pantry and the kitchen, around the corner and into the den. A power strip was plugged into the end.

This, once Dave built his safe room, was where he would hook up his microwave and coffee maker, as well as a small television, a DVD player and a floor lamp. He'd computed the wattage requirements of each item, and determined he could run all of them if he wanted to.

As long as the generator was running.

He walked into the back yard, toting his second AR-15 rifle with him. He leaned it up against the fence where he'd be working, just in case he needed it.

Then he started to dig.

In the corner of the yard, where he'd assembled the outhouse before, he took his post hole diggers and dug a hole twelve inches across and four feet deep. Once done, he took the wooden components of the outhouse and assembled it, like a large three dimensional jigsaw puzzle. He made sure that each piece was added exactly as it was the first time he'd built it, so that all of the screw holes lined up perfectly.

The final step in the process was installing the padded seat that Sarah had insisted on. He couldn't help wondering if she would ever make use of it.

And he made a vow to himself, then and there, that he would find a way to find Sarah and the girls. And if they were still alive, he would find a way, somehow, to get them back home again.

Once he was done, he went back into the house, placed two rolls of toilet paper into a watertight Tupperware container, and placed it on a shelf within easy reach of the seat.

It was late afternoon. He'd succeeded in killing most of another day. But he felt productive. He knew that as each day went by, his solitary prison would become a little bit more tolerable. It wouldn't be a easy life, living here. But he figured he'd be a lot better off than his neighbors, who hadn't done anything to prepare for doomsday.

It also occurred to him that all those times he doubted himself, all those times he thought he might be crazy for prepping for Armageddon, were just wasted emotions. He had been right about the Mayans and the EMPs.

There was no one to brag to. No one to tell, "I told you so!"

But despite the fact his whole world had gone to shit now, he still managed to take just a little bit of satisfaction in knowing he was right. And he would survive, when most others wouldn't.

–14–

He walked around the fence line, examining it closely for any cracked or broken fence pickets.

Once he was satisfied, he went back to his covered deck and opened up the first of two rabbit cages.

The girls had named each of the four rabbits, but Dave could only remember one of their names. It was light brown in color, with white paws, and his name was Thumper.

He reached inside the cage and lifted Thumper out, not knowing that Thumper didn't like to be carried.

He learned something else about Thumper too. Rabbits have sharp claws.

One thing about Dave Speer, was that he usually learned his lesson the first time. After Thumper sprang free from his arms, leaving behind a bunch of nasty scratches, Dave decided there had to be a better way.

The other male rabbit was black and white. He'd wanted to name it "Squad Car," but the girls thought that was a dumb name.

"No, it's cute. Squad car, like a police car. It's black and white, Get it?"

This time he carried the cage to the back yard and merely turned it on its side, so that the rabbit slid to the bottom and out the door. Then he righted it again as the bunny hopped off, looking for a place to hide.

Next came the second cage, which held the two female rabbits. He freed them the same way.

After all four of the rabbits were bounding about the back yard, he looked at them and smiled.

"Go forth and multiply," he told them. "Do what rabbits do best."

The rabbits were their solution to the need for long term protein in their diets.

Two years before, when they started prepping, one of the first problems they struggled with was what to do with their family pets. They had a black Labrador retriever, named Max, that Sarah had owned before she and Dave met.

Dave went to her one night and said, "We can't have a dog when the blackout hits."

"Don't you dare tell me I have to get rid of Max. He won my heart long before you did. And besides, he'll be good for chasing away looters."

"Honey, you're missing the point. A vacant house isn't supposed to have dogs. He'll bark every time someone approaches the house. He'll give us away, and everyone will know there's someone living here. And they'll know that we must have plenty of food and water, if we have enough to share with a dog."

"I don't care. Find another way."

They finally decided to compromise. Dave would not get rid of the dog, and Sarah agreed not to get another once Max died of old age. He lived another year and four months, and died peacefully in his sleep. That solved the dog problem.

Their cat, Toby, fancied himself a great lover, and roamed the neighborhood looking for ladies to romance. He'd always been that way, even when they tried to keep him inside the house. He'd lay in waiting and then bolt out the door when someone came or went, and then he'd be gone for days at a time.

One day Toby was crossing the street, on the scent of a feline in heat. He had love on his mind, and never saw the delivery truck which came barreling out of nowhere. He was flattened like a pancake, and the cat problem was solved.

Then the only problem was the girls' desire for a new pet.

Dave went to Sarah one night and said, "Let's get them some rabbits."

"Why rabbits?"

"Because rabbits are perfect. They're a great source of protein, and probably the only animal we can raise in our back yard without the neighbors knowing about them."

"Yes, but you want us to eat rabbits, of all things?"

"Well, think about it, Sugar. We'll need a source of protein to keep us strong and healthy. We can't raise chickens because the roosters crowing would alert the whole neighborhood. Rabbits multiply faster than chickens, and make no noise at all. And they eat grass. We wouldn't have to stock a lot of feed for them. During the warm weather months they can eat the grass out of the yard. We can pull up the extra grass from the Hansen's yard, put it in trash bags in the garage, and use it to feed them in the winter months when the grass isn't growing. It's perfect."

Sarah was still a little hesitant.

"But what's to keep us from having a whole yard full of rabbits before the blackout? What if they multiply so fast we can't keep up with them?"

"We'll get two of each. Two males and two females. We'll get two big cages, and put the males in one cage and the females in the other. We'll tell the girls they can take them out to play with them, but not to let the boys mingle with the girls. Then, when the stuff hits the fan, after the blackout, we'll set them all free in the back yard and let them start making babies."

"How many babies will they make, exactly?"

"They have litters, like puppies. I read on the internet that a pair of healthy adults can turn into three hundred offspring a year. Four will mean six hundred a year. They're about they size of a chicken after they're skinned. So they'll be an excellent source of protein that's absolutely renewable."

Sarah had thought for a minute and then said, "Okay, number one. I hope you don't mind catching them and skinning them, because I don't think I could bring myself to do it. Second, won't we get tired of eating rabbit every single day?"

Dave smiled.

"I will kill them and clean them and give them to you stew pot ready. And I don't think we'll get tired of them."

"Why not?"

Dave put forth his best impression of Bubba, from *Forrest Gump…*

"Well, there's rabbit stew and rabbit steaks and rabbit chili, and boiled rabbit and baked rabbit and rabbit meatloaf…"

"Uh, huh. Rabbit meatloaf?"

"Sure, why not? My point is, you're very creative when it comes to cooking, And we've included all kinds of seasonings in our stash. So no, I don't think we'll ever get tired of eating rabbit. And in reality, it's the only serious option for meat. So even if we do get tired of it, we'll eat it anyway."

She turned up her nose, but didn't say anything, so Dave went on.

"Besides, after the dust settles and the survivors start coming out, we will more than likely be the only source of meat in the neighborhood. We can barter a pair of rabbits for damn near anything. Water, ammunition, whatever we're running short of. And we can barter the meat, too. Any extra we have I can turn into jerky. And you can bet a man who hasn't had meat for several months will move heaven and earth for a bag full of jerky."

"How long do you think that'll be, Dave?"

"How long before I think people will start coming out of their houses again? I don't know. Maybe a few weeks after the blackout. Maybe a few months. It's hard to say, but I think it'll happen, eventually. I think after all the weaker people commit suicide, and the looters stop coming around because there's nothing left to loot, the survivors will see a need to band together for mutual protection. As far as how long that'll take, I haven't a clue."

"You know the girls aren't going to let you kill their pets, don't you?"

"I wasn't planning on it, sweetheart. When we buy their rabbits, we'll buy collars for all four of them. When the blackout hits and we let them get together to breed, I'll promise the girls that their pets are not for eating. They're just for making babies. We'll let them live out their lives and die of natural causes. Then we'll bury them in the back yard and have funerals for them, just like we did for Max and Toby.

"And we'll tell the girls constantly not to let themselves get attached to the baby bunnies. Because they'll all be eaten eventually."

–15–

On the weekend after they'd decided to get rabbits, Dave had gone to Home Depot and brought back four large rolls of heavy duty chicken wire.

Sarah saw him unloading it and carrying it into the back yard.

"I thought you said you wanted rabbits. You know we're not zoned for chickens. The city will confiscate them and fine us."

"Relax," he'd said. "I'm not going to build chicken coops. I'm going to bury this."

She looked at him like he was nuts.

But he was serious. And over the next seven weekends, he dug around the fence line to a depth of about a foot, three feet out from the fence. And he unrolled the three foot high fence along the hole before burying it again.

Now, with all four rabbits set free, he expected them to do two things. He expected them to dig, and he expected them to mate. He wasn't disappointed to see Thumper mount one of the females almost immediately.

As for the digging, he didn't care if they dug any burrows in the middle of the yard. He just didn't want them to do it close to the fence, where they might get out. His logic was that if they tried to dig a hole within three feet of the fence, they'd only be able to go down a foot before the heavy chicken wire stopped them dead in their furry little tracks. If that happened often enough, they might get the hint and just give up. If they didn't give up, then at least their holes would be in the center of the yard.

He took Max's old water bowl from a shelf on the back of the deck and placed it onto the deck floor. He'd keep it filled with water, so that the rabbits had a ready water source in his back yard. Another measure to discourage them from digging their way out. It would pain him to some degree to share the precious water with the rabbits. But it was an acceptable tradeoff. They would provide him with nourishment and strength for the foreseeable future. Fair is fair, after all.

The rabbits wouldn't be able to get into the Hansen yard because of the six foot privacy fence that separated the two yards. Dave, however, would need to go over there on a daily basis in the spring, to water and care for his crops. He'd need ready access in the summer, to gather fruit and nuts from their trees. And he'd need access in the fall and winter, to gather firewood from inside the Hansen house.

To solve this problem, Dave took a keyhole saw, went to the back fence and cut through the top horizontal stringer, between two of the vertical pickets.

The stringers were nothing more than two by fours that ran between the fence posts, on which the pickets were fastened.

After he cut through the top stringer, he installed a hinge to reconnect the two.

Then he did the same thing to the center and bottom stringers.

Lastly, he cut the stringers in a similar fashion four slats over, and had himself a crude gate.

After trimming the stringers a bit so they wouldn't drag, the gate swung freely and was just wide enough for Dave to squeeze through.

He put sliding bolt locks on each side of the gate, so that regardless of which side he was on, he could secure the gate and keep the rabbits from getting into the Hansen yard and eating his crops.

It was late in the afternoon now, and Dave was getting hungry again. It occurred to him that he needed to start counting his calories.

It was imperative that he count calories so that he didn't waste any food. Anything wasted would mean it would run out faster.

It would be easy to tell himself that the food stores would last him for many years. They'd stored enough dry stock to last the four of them for two years, after all, and now it was just him.

But that wouldn't do.

Because he fully expected to be reunited with his family some day.

In fact, the thought of that was really the only thing keeping him going. If he knew for sure they were dead, he'd blow his brains out and join them. But the last thing he wanted was to commit suicide, and his family find a way to get to him later on. He didn't want his daughters to find his body. So he'd press on.

He'd call it a day and go into the house to find something to eat. He'd calculate the calories for the sandwiches he'd already eaten, and wouldn't exceed two thousand calories for the day.

First, though, he needed to try out his fancy new outhouse.

–16–

Hi, honey. I wish I knew for sure that you'll find this some day. In a way, I feel ridiculous for writing. It seems strangely akin to a man sitting in solitary confinement talking to himself simply because there's nobody else around to talk to.

Eventually those men go insane, I know that. But what I don't know is whether or not it's the talking to themselves that makes them insane. Or maybe talking to themselves helps keep them sane longer.

I'm finding that putting these words on paper is somehow therapeutic. Somehow, I feel closer to you when I write to you. I know that sounds ridiculous, but hey, you always said I was a ridiculous kind of guy, right?

I've been hesitant to go into Lindsey and Beth's bedrooms. I've been afraid of how I'll feel when I go in there and smell their scents, and see their stuffed animals and other things. I know I need to do it. But I'm so afraid I'll break down and cry like a baby.

I'm determined to do that tomorrow, though. It's been six days since the blackout now, and I haven't taken a single step towards hiding our food.

I did pull out the old posters we've been collecting. I even laughed, remembering when Lindsey insisted that she wanted to throw away all of her Justin Bieber posters. I remember when you told her, "But just a few months ago you were madly in love with him." She said,

"Mommmm, that was before I grew up. I'm so over him now." And you turned to me and said, "I must have missed the memo. Since when is eleven grown up?"

I counted them. All total, including the ones currently on their walls, we have twenty two of them. I can stash quite a bit of stuff behind twenty two posters.

That's my project for the next two or three days. Actually, it may take longer than that. But that's okay. Time and loneliness are the two things I have the most of.

I saw the Castros leave yesterday. For several nights I was been able to peek out of our west window and see candles burning in their living room. It gave me some comfort, knowing they were okay. But I guess they figured they were better off moving elsewhere. I don't know where they went, or if they're coming back. I just saw them... all five of them, heading off down the street about nine yesterday morning.

They were heavily loaded with backpacks, and Julie pulled her wagon, which was loaded down with bottled water and boxes of foodstuffs.

They weren't armed. Wherever they're going, I hope they make it safely without being robbed. I know we didn't know them well, but they were quiet and never caused us any problems. All in all, they were good neighbors.

I'll keep an eye on their living room window to see if the candles start burning again. If they don't return, I'll go over there and see if there's anything I can use. I figure I can get enough firewood from the Hansen house to last at least two years, maybe three. If they're not back by then, I'll assume they're not coming back, and I'll start mining wood from their house as well.

I installed the outhouse a few days ago. It works great. I even put some Sports Illustrated magazines in there, in a waterproof container.

I know it doesn't sound very romantic, but every time I sit on that padded seat I think of you and smile. Maybe I shouldn't have told you that part.

I love you, honey. If anything ever happens to me, I hope you guys make it back and find this. At least you'll know that I never forgot you, and never stopped loving you.

Wherever you are and whatever you're doing, be safe. And kiss the girls for me. I love you all.

–17–

Dave had changed his sleeping habits because he was tired of waking up late in the morning and pissing away all of the sunshine. After that happened the third day in a row, he figured out that he just needed to go to bed earlier, right after it got dark, instead of stumbling around in the darkness trying to do things without the aid of light.

And it made sense for another reason. He was afraid to use flashlights after dark, for fear someone would see the light while walking past and know that the house was occupied. Whatever project he was working on in near total darkness, with only the moonlight and starlight coming in windows to aid him, it took several times longer than doing the same project in the daytime. So while he thought he was getting things done, he was really just spinning his wheels.

And his new sleep schedule was a resounding success. By going to bed at sundown, he was wide awake before dawn. He had time to brew himself some coffee on his campfire stove on the back deck, and watch the rabbits hopping around, eating the grass, while he planned his day. Then, as soon as the house was light enough to start work, he put his plans in motion. It worked much better than his old method of sleeping until ten or eleven, then scrambling to beat the sunset, and feeling around in the dark trying to make up for lost time.

He was awakened three different times the previous night by gunfire. The third time he saw what he thought were headlights shining into the front windows, and he got up to investigate.

Through the window he could see a house, fully engulfed in flames, two blocks away.

He looked at the treetops. Thankfully they were still.

It occurred to him then that he had no back up plan if anyone ever set *his* house on fire. With no water to put it out, he'd have to evacuate and let the house burn to the ground, with all his provisions. It was a troubling thought.

He stood at the window and watched for a time, until he was confident the fire wouldn't spread to his own street. The flames seemed to be dying down now, and neither of the houses on each side of the burning house had caught fire.

Still, it worried him enough to prevent him from falling back to sleep again.

He checked his watch. It was still an hour before sunrise.

He heard automatic gunfire coming from a few streets away, in the opposite direction from the burning house.

Most of the gunfire occurred at night. It was only sporadic during the daylight hours, but had become quite frequent in darkness.

He assumed that's because the looters thought it safer to break into homes under cover of darkness.

He also assumed that since the looters didn't know which homeowners were armed, they sometimes got surprised by homeowners wanting to protect their property.

He hoped the homeowners won such battles. And he hoped that they showed the looters no mercy.

He walked to the back door and out onto the deck. It was still too early to fire up the camping stove to make coffee. It was nothing more than a small burner that perched atop a disposable bottle of propane. But it still put out a small circle of blue flame that had enough light to be seen some distance away. No sense sending out a beacon to others who might be anxious to get such a fuel source.

It was much smarter to wait an hour and brew his coffee in the daylight.

Dave sat on a folding chair on the deck and contemplated his future. It was becoming easier now to consider the possibility that his wife and daughters may have died. If their plane was still in the air when the blackout hit, it would have lost all power and would have dropped like a rock.

He hated to think about it, but he had no choice. It was a real possibility. At least if they died that way, it would have been over rather quickly. They'd have screamed together and hugged each other and prayed. But then after the crash, they'd be at peace. They wouldn't have to worry about dying of thirst, or starving to death, or being murdered by bands of marauders taking what they wanted at gunpoint.

Then he began to wonder.

He was assuming that the airplanes would fall from the sky after the EMP. But what if that wasn't the case?

He'd been in airplanes flying through thunderstorms. He'd even looked out a window and seen a bolt of lightning hit one of the wings once.

And nothing happened.

And that made him think.

The airplane he was on didn't blow up or crash because it wasn't grounded. It was in essence a flying Faraday cage. The lightning bolt hit the plane, and the electricity encircled the outer skin and then dissipated, without harming the people inside.

He wondered… wouldn't the airplane react the same way when the EMP hit it?

Perhaps the safest place in the world to be when the EMP hit was aboard an airplane.

But then what? Even if the airplane survived, how could it land without its glide slope beacon telling it when and where to approach the airfield? How could it find its way when air traffic controllers couldn't communicate with it, and give the pilots landing instructions?

How would the pilots know whether or not it was safe to land on a particular runway, even if they could find the airport? Without the tower giving them clearance to land, they'd have no idea who or what might be sitting on the runway, or the taxiways, and in their way.

But somewhere in the recesses of his memory, Dave found a straw to grasp at. It seemed that months before, he'd watched a program on the Discovery Channel about emergency landings. And they'd talked about training for such instances. They'd talked about the FAA requiring pilots to train for landings when they lost contact with air traffic control.

They even showed commercial airline pilots, in a flight simulator, approaching a blacked out airport. And it showed as they overflew the airport, to make sure the runway was clear. Then it showed them as they circled back around, and without the aid of a glide slope beacon landed the plane the old fashioned way. By watching their instruments and looking out the windows.

On the program, the pilots were able to land safely in the simulator.

It gave Dave renewed hope that Sarah, Lindsey and Beth may have survived even if they were still in the air when the EMP hit.

By the time the sun finally rose that morning, Dave had pretty much convinced himself that his family was still intact. And even if he was dead wrong, he'd continue to believe it.

He had to. Otherwise he might as well just give up. For without the belief that he'd someday reconcile with his wife and daughters, he'd eventually go insane.

And then he'd realize there was no reason to go on. He'd blow his brains out, like he knew many others around him were doing each and every day.

He opened the valve on the small bottle of propane and struck a match to the gas. Then he filled his campfire coffee pot with water and a small amount of coffee grounds and put it atop the tiny stove to simmer.

He tried to remember how far Sarah's brother and sister in law lived from the airport in Kansas City. He'd only been to their place once, but was impressed by all of the things Tommy had showed him. They'd been prepping too now, for quite some time. Their food stores and supplies at least equaled those that Dave and Sarah had been able to gather.

By Dave's best estimate, their house was no more than twenty miles from the airport. It was certainly within two days walking distance.

If his family was able to land safely, and then was able to meet up with Tommy and Susan, there was no reason to believe that they wouldn't have been able to make it back to Tommy and Susan's house. And once there, they'd have the water, food and security they needed to survive.

Dave had a lot to do after he finished his coffee. And he'd do it with a renewed sense of purpose, and a renewed optimism.

His family was alive.

They had to be.

–18–

Having convinced himself beyond any doubt that his daughters were still alive made it easier to enter their bedrooms. He'd been dreading it, knowing the memories the rooms would bring back. But now, it didn't seem to sadden him as much.

He started in Lindsey's room first. She was his oldest. He could still vividly remember holding her in the palms of his hands on the day she was born. It was the first time he'd allowed himself to cry in Sarah's presence. He considered it unmanly. Sarah thought it was sweet.

He felt his eyes moisten now, but he'd hold the tears back. He had work to do.

He entered the room and closed the door behind him. Then he took out his frustration by punching a hole in the wall.

It felt good. He chuckled, thinking it was just what he'd needed.

But his mission wasn't to destroy the house.

Once the wall had a hole punched in it, he took a sheetrock saw he'd brought up from the garage. Using the hole he punched as a starting point, he cut a rectangular hole about a foot square between the studs.

Then he went back to the garage with a laundry basket from Lindsey's bedroom. He'd dumped her dirty laundry on the floor, but she wasn't there to call him on it. So he figured it was okay.

In the garage, he opened one of several large cardboard boxes stacked against the wall on the side of the garage they never used.

The box was full of dry food, and was way too heavy to lug up the stairs. So he filled the laundry basket and lugged it up instead.

Back in Lindsey's bedroom, he dropped the food a package at a time into the hole he'd cut in the wall, until he'd completely filled the cavity, from the floor to the bottom of the hole.

It worked quite well. He'd been able to hide thirty boxes of spaghetti noodles, several bags of dried beans and soup mix, and several bags of trail mix.

Then he took an old poster of the Backstreet Boys and hung it over the wall to cover the hole.

He stood back to admire his work. There was no way a looter would discover his stash, unless he hated the Backstreet Boys so much he took a punch at them.

And Dave imagined that looters would have more important things to worry about.

They'd planned for every contingency. One scenario they considered was that somehow someone would discover that their house wasn't vacant after all, and force their way in to loot it.

It wasn't a very likely scenario for several reasons.

First and foremost, it would mean that they'd made a mistake. That they let the smells of their cooking drift into the street. Or one of them walked past a window and was spotted. Or someone heard them talking to each other in the back yard.

And that wasn't likely. They planned to be extremely careful.

Secondly, if looters were in the house, it would mean they'd somehow gotten past Dave, and that wasn't very likely either. Dave would carry his 9 mm handgun on his side every minute of every day. And at night, he'd have it within easy reach.

He'd also have one of his AR-15s within a few yards at all times.

Sarah, also, would be armed. She wasn't a big fan of guns. But she'd use it to protect her family, and that was good enough for Dave.

Dave considered it highly unlikely, therefore, that looters would make their way into the house.

"I know it's unlikely," Sarah had said. "But we at least need to consider the possibility, just like we're considering all the others."

So they'd come up with what they considered to be a brilliant plan. They'd hide all of their food in various places around the house. In the walls and attic, mainly. Also inside the oven, behind the refrigerator and hot water heater, inside the air conditioner vents.

In the pantry, they would leave a few lonely food items out in the open. A half used box of spaghetti, a few outdated canned goods. A stale box of crackers.

And if the looters ever made it inside, they would swear up and down that there was no more food to be had. They would tell the looters, "Hey, we do the same thing you do. We go out every couple of days and steal what we can. This is all we have."

In theory, it would work, although they fully expected the looters to look around just to set their own minds at ease.

Dave had twelve knives hidden discretely around the house as well, in the event such a scenario ever happened. Behind drawers, under couch cushions, above door jambs.

When he told Sarah of his plans to do so, she asked why.

"Well, if they make it in here, that means they've somehow managed to disarm us. Which means two things. First of all, we'll be at their mercy. They can leave us unharmed, or they can kill us before they leave. Second, if they do leave us unharmed, they'll almost certainly take our weapons with them, and leave us defenseless against future looters.

"Neither option is acceptable. So if it ever gets to that point, while they're searching the house for more food I'll be trying to get to one of my hidden knives. And I won't have any problem stabbing those sons of bitches right through the heart."

Hiding food in the walls was a slow process. By the time the sun set in the evening, he had worked his way halfway through Lindsey's room. He'd only made a dent in their food stores, though. It would take him several more days to complete the project.

But he didn't mind. He'd convinced himself that his family was still alive. And, that being the case, he fully expected to reunite with them.

Someday.

Somehow.

And having made that resolution, he knew that he wasn't just going through all this trouble for his own benefit.

He was doing it for them.

-19-

Hi, honey.

It's been a few days since I've written. I hope you haven't missed me too much.

Yes, that was a joke. A lame one, sure, but it's the best I can do under the circumstances.

It's been almost two weeks since the blackout. I was putting hash marks on the calendar so I could keep track of which day it was, but there have been a couple of times when I might have forgotten.

I've been wearing myself out on purpose so I'd sleep better at night and not have as much time to lay here and miss you guys and feel sorry for myself.

The gunshots are happening more and more frequently now. I think that people are getting more and more desperate as they're running out of food in their pantries. I'd like to think that the homeowners are winning the battle against the looters, but then it occurs to me that even the homeowners will probably turn into looters themselves if they get desperate enough.

Across the street and two houses to the west, I heard a shootout two nights ago. I looked out the following morning and saw a body laying at the end of the driveway.

It's still there. There's a blood trail leading from the front door. They dragged him from either the front porch or from inside the house.

I assume it's the body of a looter, shot by the homeowner.

At first, I was puzzled and wondered why they didn't just bury him in their back yard. I mean, it's not like they're gonna bring an ambulance to pick up the body and take it away. It kind of pissed me off, to be honest. I figured it'll lay out there and decompose and stink up the whole neighborhood.

But then the more I thought about it, the more I decided it's a brilliant move. I think our neighbor is sending a message to other looters that he is armed and does not play. And that if other looters don't stay away, they'll end up the same way. Talk about a very effective message.

I've been watching a lot of home movies lately. I'm running my generator about an hour and a half a day, always in the daytime. While it's running, I take a break from working and eat my lunch, and watch the videos on the small TV from the Faraday cage. Today I watched Beth's first soccer game. I caught myself smiling when she went the wrong way and kicked the ball into her own goal. Then she jumped up and down, all proud of herself because she didn't realize what she'd done.

I miss the little angel. I miss all of you.

You may think this is really bizarre, and it probably is, but a couple of days ago I picked up one of your scarves and held it to my face.

It still smelled of you, and I closed my eyes and pretended you were there with me. I don't know what type of perfume it was, but it was very comforting.

I know, that's weird, but I don't think I liked it because I'm crazy or anything. I hope you don't think so either.

I think I liked it because, well, it made me feel just a tiny bit closer to you.

I took the same scarf and tied it around my bed pillow. I know the scent will eventually fade away, but in the meantime I think it's helping me sleep better. Like maybe my subconscious mind thinks you're there beside me while I sleep.

Whatever it is, I've been sleeping much better since I started sleeping with your scarf.

I look forward to the day when I have you next to me for real. I hope and pray that's not just a pipe dream.

Kiss the girls for me and tell them I love them.

–20–

He was finished hiding his provisions now. Most of it was stashed within the walls in the upstairs rooms. The rest was in the attic, hidden beneath the blown in insulation, and at various other hiding places throughout the house.

Dave was still working to empty the chest freezer in the garage. He hadn't touched the dry stock yet.

Running the freezer for only an hour and a half per day was preserving the food, as he'd hoped it would. He figured that before the blackout, the freezer's condenser probably ran off and on for just a couple of hours a day.

Now, running off the generator, it ran constantly for the entire ninety minutes or so that the generator was running. The food in the freezer was no longer frozen solid as a rock, but it was icy and would last until he ate it all.

He couldn't help but chuckle at his strange new diet.

Sarah had always been a stickler when she prepared their meals. She always made sure that they had a meat, a vegetable and a carbohydrate. Always, without exception.

The girls had grown up having three things on their plates. Meatloaf, masked potatoes and stewed spinach. Or pork chops, macaroni and cheese, and sliced carrots.

Always three things.

Dave, on the other hand, didn't care what he ate, as long as he got the two thousand calories he needed each day to preserve his strength.

And he was determined not to let any of the food go to waste. So one day he might eat an entire three pound bag of frozen broccoli and cheese, and the next day he might eat half a bag of frozen chicken wings.

Most of the food packages had their calorie counts right on the package, so all he had to do was a little bit of math. Once he determined what would equal two thousand calories, he cooked it all the same way. In a sauce pan over his small camp stove. It didn't matter what it was… frozen vegetables, fish fillets, onion rings. It all got simmered in the pan, with just a little bit of Wesson oil to keep it from sticking.

There was nothing sophisticated about Dave Speer. He sucked at cooking or keeping a tidy house. He'd always been that way. Sarah would be aghast at his eating habits now.

But in his mind, it didn't matter. With Sarah gone, food was no longer something to enjoy or savor. It was merely something to keep his body functioning.

No more, no less.

To stretch his food as far as possible, he'd eat the things that would spoil first. That's why he was working on the freezer.

After the frozen food was gone, he'd work on the canned goods next. His goal was get rid of all the cans before winter came around again. Except the spaghetti sauce, tuna fish and Vienna sausages.

His logic was sound. They'd experimented a lot with various types of foods in the two years leading up to the blackout.

Dave always volunteered to be the guinea pig. They would test various canned goods by putting them into the chest freezer for a couple of weeks until they froze solid. Then they'd thaw them out again, and Dave would eat them to see if they were tainted.

They found that most of the cans expanded at least a little. Those cans with a lot of water, like green beans and sweet corn, expanded a lot.

In fact, both of those items expanded to the point where the cans broke open in the freezer.

It didn't make too much of a mess. The contents of the can were a very thick and icy goo at that point. But it did convince Dave and Sarah that storing large quantities of canned corn and green beans would be a bad idea.

Conversely, they found that certain other items froze and thawed extremely well. Among them were jellied cranberry sauce, which everyone in the house loved and which would satisfy their desire for sweet foods, condensed soups, Vienna sausages, beef stew and tuna fish.

The tuna packed in oil, anyway. Tuna packed in water swelled considerably and even Dave was afraid to eat it.

After they'd determined which canned items could be frozen and thawed and were still safe to eat, they knew where to focus their hoarding efforts.

Dave worked part time at the cabinet shop not because he had to. They could have survived easily without the part time job. He took the job at the cabinet shop for the express purpose of funding their prepping efforts.

And every time he got paid, he visited the local Walmart to stock up on canned goods, dry goods, ingredients for trail mix and frozen meat.

The meat was cooked and then slowly dried in the oven until it was shelf stable. The idea was to soak it in water later on to soften and rehydrate it, and serve it in gravies or stews.

Now, Dave's game plan was simple.

First, he'd eat the rest of the food in the freezer. Then, he'd eat the canned items that he knew would be ruined if they were still around when winter returned. Then he'd eat the other canned goods; the ones that would survive a freeze and still be good.

Lastly, he'd eat the dry goods, like the spaghetti noodles, macaroni and cheese, dry beans and trail mix. He could live off of those indefinitely.

During the late summer and fall, he'd augment his diet with fruits and vegetables he planned to grow in the large back yard of the Hansen house, and fruit and nuts from their trees.

He hoped to be able to grow enough to put aside over the winter months

And all year around, he'd enjoy rabbit stew. Once all the canned meats and trail mix was gone, it would become his primary source of protein.

Dave went out and looked at the sky. It was the middle of March now. He never was much of a gardener. Sarah was quite good at growing things, and he'd assumed she would be around to tell him what to do. It was another dreadful mistake.

He'd have to muddle through without her, and hope for the best.

He had enough common sense, though, to avoid making even more blunders. Like, for example, he knew that San Antonio occasionally had a late freeze in March. He'd therefore wait until April, when it was no longer cold at night, before he'd start his planting. He didn't want to get his crops in the ground only to watch them freeze to death.

With the planting delayed for a few more weeks, he had only one major project left.

He'd spend the next few days building his safe room.

–21–

Dave realized he should have built his safe room long before. It was an essential part of his survival. If Sarah and the girls had been here, it would have taken precedence over some of the other things... the outhouse, the generator, securing the food.

But now, all of those other projects were done. It was time to tackle this one.

And there was a bit of added incentive as well. The day before, he'd walked around the perimeter of his yard, making sure that the rabbits weren't trying to dig their way out. A small hole in the fence caught his eye.

It was perfectly round and fresh. A bullet hole made the night before.

He had no clue where it came from.

He was certain he wasn't the target, though. No one in their right mind would waste a bullet on a fence. He'd heard several gunshots the previous night, and some were fairly close.

He assumed it was a stray bullet that was meant for someone else, and found his fence instead.

The bullet came through the fence at a steep angle, and probably embedded itself in the dirt of his yard. He guessed a 9 mm, based on the size of the hole, and was tempted to look for the bullet to see if he was right.

But then he decided he had more important things to do.

If the bullet had come in from a different direction, at a different angle, it would have penetrated his house instead of the fence.

And that would be a problem.

The number of gunshots he was hearing each night, and sometimes during the daytime, had been increasing. There were more and more people out there who were getting more and more desperate. The chances of stray bullets finding the house would be getting greater by the day.

Eventually the shooting would subside, Dave figured. Eventually all of the looters would be dead. Or the homeowners. Eventually the only shots he'd hear would be from the people who had given up and couldn't take it any more.

But he had no idea how long that would be.

The safe room wouldn't be an easy thing to build. Half inch plywood wasn't light, and it was clumsy as hell when you tried to maneuver it through a house. Moreover, by the time he lugged all eighty sheets of it from the garage to the den, he'd likely have no strength left to build it.

The solution was to build it over the course of several days.

He'd start with the west wall of the house. That was the side he'd found the bullet hole, and the side he considered most vulnerable.

It was also the only side of his safe room that had only the exterior wall between it and the outside. The other three sides had interior walls and furniture to help stop bullets.

He moved the dining room set into the garage and put it behind the generator box. It was the only way he could swing the plywood in the dining room to make the turn into the den.

When he picked up the first sheet of plywood, he realized how tough this job was going to be.

It wasn't just the weight. He had to pick it up in the middle, his arms stretched four feet apart, and balance it so that the corners didn't hit the floor and get damaged. Moreover, he had to walk sideways through the doorways.

It only took him one sheet to realize there had to be a better way. By the time he got the first sheet to the den, he was exhausted and had to stop and rest. And even worse, his back ached something fierce.

He knew if he threw his back out, he wouldn't be able to finish the project for days, if not weeks. And that would mean he'd be vulnerable for a lucky bullet any time, day or night.

He'd been afraid to do any more damage to the house. It was bad enough he'd had to punch holes in the bedroom walls upstairs. As essential as it was, it still pained him to do it.

They'd redone the kitchen right after they bought the house. Sarah had picked out the cabinets and floor tile and loved them. She said the kitchen was her favorite part of the house. The one thing she'd stressed to him when he'd laid out his plans for the safe house was an admonition:

"Dave, don't you dare damage my kitchen floors when you bring in that plywood."

But Sarah was no longer here.

Screw the kitchen floors.

By late afternoon, he'd brought in ten sheets of plywood by dragging them through the kitchen, and laid them in a stack on the floor of the den.

The kitchen tiles were scarred now, and he'd even managed to chip a couple of them. The carpet in the den was frayed as well, and was pulled up from the tack strip where the kitchen tile transitioned to carpet.

But it couldn't be helped.

He'd gladly weather the wrath of Sarah just to have her back.

And he continued to hold out hope that he would, someday, somehow.

Once he'd finished bringing in the ten sheets of plywood, he was exhausted. He laid on the couch that he'd moved out of the way and against the wall to make room for the plywood, intending to close his eyes and rest for a few minutes.

He woke up four hours later. It was nearing midnight now, and dark outside.

"Oh, crap!" he muttered to himself, and started to get up. But every muscle in his body screamed at him. He was stiff and sore and exhausted.

And he began to wonder if two thousand calories a day was enough to sustain him.

He'd never remembered being this tired before. Was it possible that his body wasn't getting enough fuel? That he was slowly letting himself wear down? He'd noticed his clothes were considerably looser than they used to be. He didn't see that as a problem, though. He, like many other men in their late 30s, had a few extra pounds to lose.

But now, he was starting to wonder. And he was missing the days when he could just jump on the internet to find an answer to his questions.

In the end, he made two decisions. One was that, as guilty as he felt for falling asleep on duty, he wouldn't drag any more plywood tonight. There was sufficient moonlight coming through the windows to enable him to do so, but he didn't want to overstress his body more than he already had.

Instead, he merely leaned five of the sheets he'd already brought in against the outer wall of the den. Then he pushed the couch in front of them. He'd spend the night here tonight, confident that the two and a half inches of plywood would stop any bullets coming in from the outer wall.

He hoped that bullets coming from any other direction would be stopped by the interior walls and furniture around him.

The second decision he made was to modify his calorie count. When he was working major projects, that required a lot of strength, he'd increase his calorie count to 2500 calories a day. He hoped the extra five hundred calories would give him the extra boost he needed to get through the heavy projects.

He could compensate by cutting his count down to 1900 between major projects, when he was mostly sitting around watching the world go by.

Once his safe room was built, he expected to be able to relax a bit. The only major projects he had planned for the foreseeable future were planting his crops, and then harvesting them later on.

Both the planting and the harvesting would have to be done by hand.

And neither would be fun.

Dave popped three Motrin and laid on the couch, expecting his screaming muscles to keep him awake while he waited for the medicine to take effect.

But he was asleep within seconds. His exhausted body just refused to function any longer.

–22–

It occurred to Dave when he woke up around noon that the hardest thing he'd do today would be getting up off the couch. Every muscle he had, including those he didn't even know he had, were stiff and sore. Every one of them rebelled against the movement, and he had to fight the pain just to get to his bottle of Motrin and the bottle of water across the room.

After he walked around for a few minutes, he started to loosen up. He was still very tired. But he'd fight his way through the pain.

The actual construction part of the safe room was easy, compared to dragging the plywood in. The plywood was eight feet tall when stood on its end. The exact height of the ceiling.

It was a snug fit as he leaned each sheet of plywood up against the outer wall, because of the carpet and padding laid upon the concrete floor. The weight of the plywood compressed them to about half an inch in thickness, which meant the top of the plywood dragged against the ceiling.

Dave had to pound the top of the wood to make it stand upright, but once it was in place it wasn't in danger of falling.

But he went an extra step anyway, by screwing a piece of pre-drilled two by two wood into the ceiling in front of the wood.

The first piece of the wall was complete. He took the second five sheets of plywood he'd dragged in the day before and stood them up next to the first five, securing them the same way.

Then he took a break and ate before he started dragging more wood in.

By late afternoon he had the next five sheets in the den. The going was a bit easier this time, because he was pacing himself now. Instead of working non stop to move as many pieces as he could before he lost daylight, he was taking a rest break after every sheet.

It seemed to work much better.

With the west wall completed, he turned the corner and used the next five sheets to start the north wall of the structure. Like before, the plywood was held snugly in place by the ceiling. But again, Dave took the added step of bracing it into place.

He went to bed that night with bulletproof protection on two sides of the couch, four more sheets of plywood laying on the floor, and a bit less sore than the previous night.

It took Dave four more days to finish the safe room. Once completed, it was a structure eight feet high, twelve feet long, and eight feet wide. One of the walls was built around the fireplace and had the added protection of four layers of brick, in addition to the plywood.

The fireplace didn't mean much now, as temperatures inside the safe room grew to a stuffy eighty degrees in the afternoons.

But in the wintertime, Dave had in essence constructed himself a windowless cabin, inside the house, with walls that were at least two and a half inches thick. The east wall, which faced the interior of the house, included a door about thirty inches wide and five feet high. He made it short on purpose, to help keep the winter heat in. Across the doorway he'd hung a wooden rod, fashioned by cutting a broomstick in half. And across the broomstick was a shower curtain from the downstairs bathroom he'd emptied out on the first day after the blackout. Back when he was trying to make the house appear to be vacant.

He stood back and admired his work.

Something appeared to be missing, but he couldn't figure out what it was.

And finally, in a moment of fancy, Dave decided to provide a name for his creation.

He took a can of black spray paint from his garage and sprayed the words "THE HOLE" over the small doorway.

"I christen thee 'the hole' after the scummiest and loneliest place in every prison movie ever made. I am now officially in solitary confinement."

He had no bottle of champagne to break across the bow of his new home. So instead he doused the painted words with water from a small bottle of Ozarka.

Then he guzzled the rest of the bottle, stood back and laughed.

For the rest of the day, he lay in the middle of the hole curled up in the fetal position, wondering if he was going mad.

-23-

Happy birthday, honey. You're thirty six today. In a different time, in a different world, I'd have cooked you breakfast in bed this morning. Then, since it's Saturday, or at least I think it is, I'd have crawled into bed with you and made sweet love to you.

This stinks. All of it. Instead of helping you ring in another year of your life I'm sitting here cursing the stench of death all around me.

One of the neighbors killed a looter a couple of weeks ago and left his body on the street to rot. Every couple of days I've stood at the window and watched the buzzards slowly pick the meat off the bones. Lately I've worn one of the paper masks from our first aid kit whenever I'm outside. The stench is that bad.

Yesterday I saw a stray dog tear off one of the looter's forearms and carry it away like a trophy. I wish he'd have taken the whole damn thing.

I've been waiting for the birds and the dogs to finish picking the meat off of it. I figured when it was just bones, it wouldn't smell so bad. And then it occurred to me that the smell of death is all around me no matter which way the wind is blowing.

I'm surrounded by death. I suppose there are suicides in a lot of the houses in the neighborhood now, slowly rotting away. Seeing that desperate dog reminded me that I haven't heard any barking at night lately. Remember when we used to lay in bed and bitch about all the neighbors' dogs having barking contests at three in the morning? I haven't heard a dog bark in two weeks or more, and in fact the one I saw picking at the looter's carcass was the only one I've seen since the blackout began.

I suppose they were probably shot by owners who could no longer feed or water them.

Either that, or they starved to death.

I've been trying to remember everything I could about Tommy and Susan's house. I know it wasn't in a crowded neighborhood like our place is. I seemed to remember it was a bit outside the city. I hope you and the girls are being spared the awful smells.

Now for some good news. I've finished the safe room and christened it "the hole." In prison movies that's what they call solitary confinement. I figured it was appropriate. When I bring you guys back here later on we can rename it. And yes, I do plan on bringing you guys back here some day. I don't know how or when, but it'll happen. You can bank on it.

A little more good news. It dawned on me that since the chest freezer in the garage survived, some other things might have also. So I went around and started plugging all of the appliances into the generator cord one at a time. It turns out that everything that was plugged into the wall is shot. But there were a few items in the attic that survived. I guess because they weren't plugged in. Anyway, we have two electric box fans, two floor lamps and a space heater up there that we can use, in addition to the stuff in the Faraday cage.

My first project tomorrow is to furnish the hole. I'm going to bring down the single bed from Beth's room and put it in there, as well as the coffee table and one of the occasional chairs from the den. The small folding table from the garage will hold the microwave and the Mr. Coffee. I'll put the DVD player and the TV on the coffee table.

I'll use the floor lamp when the generator is working and open the shower curtain when it's not. If I need to, I can burn candles to see at night, but I plan to do my sleeping during the hours of darkness.

I think when I'm done it'll resemble a college dorm room more than anything else. It'll be cramped and cozy. But at least it'll offer me some nice creature comforts for an hour and a half a day.

I screwed up big time. Yesterday I woke up in the morning and it was raining, and I kicked myself in the ass because I haven't set up my rain collection system yet.

It's not a major crisis. I counted the number of bottles I was able to fill from the tap. There were a hundred and twenty six of them. They're taking up most of the spare floorspace in the garage and in the upstairs bathroom. And I'm still drinking from the cases of bottled water we stashed, so I'm not in danger of running out. But there are still at least three hundred more empty bottles in the attic I can fill with rainwater and use to irrigate the wheat and corn crops. The rain seems to have cleared off now, but my second project is to hang the gutters and the tarps so I can be ready the next time it rains.

I've also decided to hang an extra set of gutters on the Hansen house. I think I'll have enough pieces left over. If I don't, I can fasten some two by fours to the roof to channel the water to the corners of the house and then into the trash cans below. Might as well make use of that house. They'll never be back to use it again.

I wish you were here to tell me when to start planting. I looked at the seeds in our seed stock. Most of the little packages have instructions on when and how to plant, so I should be covered on those. It's the bulk wheat and corn seed we bought on-line that I'm worried about. Neither one came with instructions, and those are our subsistence crops.

I'll keep you posted on that.

Kiss the girls for me. I love you all.

–24–

Dave awoke early the next morning, a few minutes before sunrise. It occurred to him that his body clock was starting to adjust to his sleep schedule now. That somehow his subconscious brain knew he needed to be up to take advantage of the daylight hours.

He stumbled out of bed and stretched. It was moving day today. He'd decided that after he finished furnishing the hole he'd reward himself by cranking the generator and watching a movie. Not home movies, of the girls as they were growing up. As much as he loved watching those movies, they made his heart hurt.

No, today he'd pop in an old cowboy movie. Dave was a big fan of John Wayne. As a boy, he sat on the couch in the evenings eating popcorn with his father, watching John Wayne shoot it out with the bad guys. His father was a big fan of the Duke himself, and although he preferred Wayne's war movies, he knew that Dave was more fond of the cowboy movies. So that's what the two of them watched most of the time.

When Dave's dad died, he inherited the extensive collection of western movies. He seldom watched them, but today, with all the death and misery going on in the world, he needed something to distract him from his pain.

He went to the garage and selected the tools he'd need to dismantle Beth's bed. Then he walked into her room and took the single mattress, threw it over his shoulder, and carried it down the stairs.

He was startled to discover he could smell the scent of her shampoo on the sheets.

Momentarily, he wept just a bit. Then he shook his head to bring himself back to reality.

There would be time to cry later if he wanted to. Right now he had a job to do.

Two hours later he was finished. The bed was reassembled on one wall in the hole, and all of the other gadgets were placed around the room.

He was surprised that he still had a bit of space to move around. But they had designed the small room to accommodate four, after all, so it made sense he'd still have a bit of breathing room.

Just as he'd suspected, the hole looked a lot like a college dorm room, a mish mash of "stuff" and an unmade single bed. But it was what it was. And what it was for the foreseeable future was his home. Or at least the part of his home he'd spend most of his time in.

Because of the way the hole was situated, with its single narrow door facing the interior of the house, he knew he could power the floor lamp, even at night if he wanted to, without the light being visible from outside the house. And he knew that plywood made excellent insulation, both from temperatures and from sound. He knew that the five layers of plywood would absorb the sounds from his television.

Lastly, he knew that he'd look forward to the hour and a half respite he'd be able to take from the ugliness of the world outside each day. For those precious ninety minutes, he'd be able to escape reality, watch a movie, relax a bit and feel normal again.

It was time for his break. He went to the garage and opened up his chest freezer. Most of the frozen food was gone now, and he was running out of choices.

He picked up a box of corn dogs and looked at the back. One hundred and eighty calories apiece. He closed the freezer door and took them to the kitchen, where he put eleven corn dogs on a dinner plate. They pretty much covered every inch of it.

He did the math in his head. Eleven corn dogs equaled 1980 calories. It was damn close to the 1900 calories he'd set as his goal each day. Close enough.

He wasn't crazy about corn dogs. And he knew he couldn't eat eleven at one sitting. But he only had a ninety minute window to cook them, so he'd cook them all at once, eat what he could, and save the rest for later.

Back in the garage, he placed the box back into the chest freezer and did a quick survey of what was left in it.

Another week's worth, he decided. Then he'd transition from frozen food to the canned goods that were in the cupboard. He wasn't looking forward to them. He knew that the vitamins they provided were important to his health, sure. The problem was that canned vegetables were relatively low in calories. So he might have to eat six cans of corn and peas and lima beans in a single day just to get the calories he needed to keep going.

And for a man who wasn't particularly fond of canned vegetables, that just didn't appeal to him.

The other alternative, of course, was just not eating the vegetables. But then they would eventually go bad and would expire.

To waste food under the present circumstances would be a sin. And Dave was many things, but he wasn't a sinner.

He poured a cup of gas into the generator and fired it up, then made sure the door leading into the house was completely closed.

Then he went back to the hole, put the plate of corn dogs into the microwave for two minutes, and pressed the start button.

While he was waiting for the microwave to shut off, he looked through the stack of John Wayne DVDs he'd put in the corner of the small room.

He put *Red River* aside. He remembered the Wayne character as being too mean, and he wanted something a little lighter.

He also bypassed *The Searchers*, knowing it would hit too close to home. *McClintock* wouldn't work either. Too funny.

Dave finally decided on *Rio Bravo*. A classic, and one of his favorites as a kid. He loved the way the Duke interacted with the Dean Martin and Ricky Nelson characters. He liked that there was a little bit of music in the movie, and recalled having a crush on Angie Dickinson as a kid.

He chuckled, remembering how his father paid rapt attention to the television whenever Angie Dickinson appeared wearing a black corset. It never dawned on him at the time, but perhaps his father was enamored by her too.

As he put the movie in and pressed play, the bell on the microwave announced that it was finished. Dave took the plate out, shoved a thumb into one of the corn dogs, and decided they needed to cook a bit longer. He rearranged them and punched two more minutes into the keypad.

Then he sat on his bed to wait, while listening to Dean Martin croon the opening theme to the movie.

For the next ninety minutes, he'd try his best to forget the world outside, and go back to the days of his youth. The world was a far better place back then.

–25–

Dave dozed off just before the climactic shootout and missed the end of the movie. He woke up an hour later to find the television darkened, and two houseflies sitting on two of the five corn dogs left on his plate.

"Dammit," he said while shooing the flies away. He put the dogs into a zip lock bag and left them on top of the microwave for later.

He went to the back yard, where he'd taken the ladder and sections of rain gutter the evening before, and set to work.

Like the outhouse and generator box, the gutters had been pre-fitted along the back eave of the house. All the holes had already been drilled, and it was just a matter of holding the pieces into place while screwing in the wood screws that would hold it into place.

Sarah had been around to help him during the pre-fit, and Dave was worried that it might be difficult without a second person to help. But it was actually a piece of cake. He simply left one end on the ground while he pulled the other end over the first hole, then screwed it loosely into place. Once the first screw was in place, he was able to lift the gutter up and screw the opposite end into place, then insert the additional screws between the two ends.

It helped that the aluminum gutter was very light and very flexible. Old fashioned galvanized steel gutter would have been a lot harder to deal with.

The new gutter system drained on each corner of the back of the house. He installed two down spouts that didn't go all the way to the ground. Rather, they terminated about four feet above the ground.

Beneath each downspout, he placed a fifty gallon Hefty trash can. Each can had a snap-on lid, which he'd remove the next time it looked like rain.

Dave was aware that the rainwater pouring off the roof and into these containers would carry tiny bits of the asphalt shingles as well as chemical residue. But that was okay. He had no plans to drink this water. Oh, he could in a pinch, by boiling it and using it only if he had to. But his plan was to use this water only for irrigation for his crops. His drinking water would also come from the sky, but would never touch the roof.

Once he was finished, he stepped back and admired his work. It looked good, and during a heavy rainstorm both of the trash cans would be filled within twenty minutes.

But he wouldn't stop there. He spent the next hour hanging additional gutter on the end of the covered deck. He'd built the deck himself, and had covered it with a corrugated steel roof. Rainwater typically ran down the grooves in the steel and fell off the end of the roof into the lawn below. But not anymore. Now it would be captured and channeled into a third Hefty can.

Once the gutters were up, Dave counted the extra pieces he had left. He had enough to line the back of the Hansen house as well.

He knew he could use two by fours to set up a makeshift runoff system at the Castro house next door if the family didn't return. When he'd seen them leave he was conflicted. Half of him wanted to pray for them and wish them well on whatever journey they were going on, and to see them return safely at a later time.

The other half of him, the selfish side, was hoping it was a one way trip and that they'd never be back. Because even though they would surely leave no food behind, he might be able to make use of other things. Chiefly, he could use the back of their house as an additional water source.

He took a break and sat on a folding chair on the deck. The afternoons were getting much warmer now. He'd start planting crops soon, but not just yet. He wanted to build his water supply first. It wouldn't do to start growing things just to have them die from thirst because he didn't have enough water to irrigate them. He could use some of the drinking water he'd saved from the faucet if he had to, but it had to provide for his own needs as well.

No, the smart thing to do would be to wait until after the next hard rain, fill all the barrels and empty bottles, and then plant. By then, the odds of a late freeze would be gone too. It was still cool at night, and some mornings Dave wore a windbreaker until the sun was high in the sky. Just as tragic as planting crops before he had enough water, only to watch them wither and die, would be the chance a late freeze would kill them.

He'd wait a couple or three more weeks before he planted anything. Just to be safe.

As he rested, he watched the rabbits frolicking in the yard, and happened to see Thumper riding one of the females.

"Go ahead, you old rascal. You're making my supper in a few months. It'll be nice when there are enough of you guys to allow me to just come out here and grab one of you by the ears and wring your little necks. One by one. You'll make some pretty good stew."

Then it occurred to him that Thumper was getting more sex than he was, and it made him a tad bit jealous.

Even after all the years that he and Sarah had been married, she was still the most beautiful woman he knew. And the only one he desired.

He missed her in a lot of ways. But one of the biggest things he missed was picking her up, giggling in anticipation, then carrying her to the bedroom. They were a good fit in every way. Sexually too. And he missed the feel of her naked body next to his. He missed giving her pleasure, and getting it in return. And he missed the way she lay on his chest, breathless, when it was over, telling him how much she loved him.

Once again, he had to shake the thoughts from his head. That kind of thinking would only make him miserable.

And he already had enough problems to deal with.

He looked at his watch. He'd forgotten to wind it again. It was stopped at just past nine o'clock. It was way past morning, and long before dark. Dammit.

From the position of the sun, he figured he had maybe three hours or so of daylight left. That should be plenty of time to get the post holes dug and the posts set.

He looked around, and discovered that winding his watch wasn't the only thing he'd forgotten. He'd left the post hole diggers in the garage when he pulled out the other materials.

Dammit. He wondered if the stress was getting to him.

It had been a full three hours now since the generator ran out of fuel and died. In all likelihood, the carbon dioxide fumes in the garage had already dissipated, escaping through the cracks in and around the overhead doors.

But just to be safe, he'd try to avoid breathing the fumes. He paused in the pantry, picked up his flashlight and turned it on. Then he took a deep breath, held it, and walked into the garage.

–26–

The holes had been pre-dug many months before and then filled back in. It was just another way Dave and Sarah had planned ahead to make it easier on them when the world went black. They'd installed screws on the top rail of the fence on both the east and west sides of the yard. Then they attached one long side of the rain tarps onto the fence rail by merely placing the metal grommets over the screws.

Once one side of the tarp was attached to the fence, it was just a matter of rolling the tarp out to see where they needed to place the posts. And once that was done, Dave had used the post hole diggers to dig the holes, twenty four inches deep.

There were two holes for each tarp, on opposite sides of the yard. They were twelve feet away from the fence, and nineteen feet apart from each other.

The idea was to stretch the 12 by 20 foot tarp completely out, to catch as much rainfall as possible, but to leave a slight crease on the middle of the open side, to allow all the water to channel to the center, and then run off in the same spot.

For that to happen, there needed to be just a little slack on the open side. That's why they dug the post holes nineteen feet apart, instead of twenty. Whenever it rained, they would hang up the tarps on each side of the yard, roll them out and connect them to the tops of the posts. Then they'd take a Hefty can and place it below the crease, so the water landing on the tarps would fall into the can instead of into the yard.

Once the water was in the can, the idea was to take the empty soda bottles and submerge them beneath the water level to fill them, then to cap them and put them aside. Dave would work the trash can on one side of the yard and Sarah would work the one on the other side, so they could stay ahead of both trash cans and keep them from overflowing. Lindsey and Beth would feed them the empty bottles and take away the full ones.

That had been the plan, anyway. Now that he'd be working alone, Dave would have to modify the plan a little bit, and would likely still have a hard time preventing the cans from overflowing and losing precious water during a heavy rain.

But he'd find a way.

He took the post hole diggers to the spots where he'd dug the four holes months before and then refilled with the loose dirt. The reason he'd pre-dug the holes was so that the dirt wouldn't be packed and would come out easily. Having to pound the diggers into hard packed ground would make noise, and could draw attention. It was the last thing he needed.

Thus far, as far as he knew, he was successful in carrying out the ruse that his house was vacant. He didn't want to do anything to change that.

As he removed the loosened dirt from the holes and set it aside, he noticed one of the female rabbits watching him.

"No, I'm not digging a hole for you. Don't even think about it."

Then he felt sheepish and looked around, to make sure no one had seen him talking to a rabbit.

Then he felt doubly stupid, knowing full well that no one could see him.

Once he dug all the loose dirt out of the first hole, he placed one of the four fence posts into it, letting it fall all the way to the bottom. Then he opened up three bags of Sacrete and poured it into the hole around the post.

The Sacrete was premixed concrete. It was a mixture of cement and gravel, and only required water to set. Once water was added, it would slowly dry and the post would become a permanent fixture in the yard.

It would have very easy for Dave to take two or three of the bottles of water he'd filled from the tap, and to pour them onto the Sacrete.

But Dave had other ideas.

Water was much too precious to waste in such a manner. So instead, he took one by twos and fastened them to the base of the post to keep it upright.

The same rain that would allow Dave to fill the rest of the empty soda bottles would also mix with the Sacrete. Then it would dry, and by the time the second rainfall came around, the posts would be sturdy enough to remove the braces.

By the time Dave finished placing the third post, the female rabbit had lost interest in what the stupid human was doing and had moved on to another part of the yard to munch on grass.

Once again, Dave was all alone in the world.

-27-

Hi Baby. I hope you and the girls are well and not worrying too much about me. I've decided that worrying about you just depresses me and stresses me out, so I've decided not to do it anymore. I know that you arrived safely, I know that Tommy and Susan were there to pick you up, and I know that Tommy is capable of getting you all back to their place safely. So worrying about you is just a wasted emotion.

Instead, I try to spend my time thinking about the day we'll be together again.

I was looking through all of the stuff you printed off the internet over the last few months. You never got around to sorting it all out, like you'd planned on doing. But that was okay. Actually, it was good, because I came across all kinds of other stuff I can use. Like planting schedules for wheat and corn.

That wasn't what I was looking for, though. What I was looking for were maps, in the event we ever had to bug out and try to make our way to Tommy and Susan's place. And once again, you didn't let me down. I found the map between the first aid procedures and the recipe for making sourdough bread in the campfire oven. Which, by the way, I've been wanting to try ever since. I figure this is a good time to do it, since the stench of the decaying bodies will surely cover up the smell of bread baking in the back yard.

Anyway, now that I have the map, I can make firm plans to come and get you guys at some point in the future. I don't know when, exactly. I think it's too risky right now. I hope that eventually, when all the shooting dies down, it'll be an indication that the world has become a safer place. And that maybe all of the looters will have been shot like the guy out there on the street.

Of course, when it gets to that point, it could also mean that the good guys are all dead, and the thugs don't have anybody left to shoot anymore.

In any event, it'll take me several weeks to get to you, traveling at night and having to stop frequently to forage for food.

It'll take even longer to bring you back. We'll have to move more slowly and cautiously with the girls.

I checked the box of parts and I'm confident it's got everything I need to get my Explorer started. Of course, it'll take a little bit of work, and I'll have to work at night, but I tested the night vision goggles and they work quite well. It'll be a little bit odd, working on a car when everything is all green. But the alternative is working on it during the daytime and risking somebody trying to take it away from me as soon as I get it started.

I'm trying not to get my hopes up that I can even get it going. In theory, I can, by bypassing or replacing all the electronic components. But I'm not going to take anything for granted. You not being here broke me of that habit. It's the only thing we didn't have a contingency plan for, and

I'm kicking myself in the ass every day. I shouldn't have let you guys go without me. My place is by your side, and I feel that I let you down.

Even if I can't get the Explorer running, I'm still coming for you. I figure ten miles a night, maybe twelve, with every third night off so I can forage for food and water. I can walk and make it in four months, maybe five.

It would be a small price to pay to see you again.

But I'd much rather drive. It'll be faster.

–28–

Dave was working in the Hansens' back yard two weeks later, digging up the grass with a long handled shovel. One shovel full at a time, he was turning the dirt over to clear the grass and weeds from the soil..

It was his second pass through.

He'd finished turning over the entire yard a couple of days before. Then he went through it with a garden rake, raking what he could of the grass and roots. Once he had them in a pile, he'd let them dry out, and then put them in trash bags and store them in his garage. It would serve as rabbit food during the winter, when the grass was scarce.

San Antonio usually had very mild winters, and the grass seldom went completely dormant. Even an occasional freeze was only temporary, and the thickest parts of the lawn somehow managed to stay green. But the growth of the grass slowed to a trickle during the cold weather months. Dave was afraid it might not be enough to sustain the growing rabbit population. So he'd build up a good supply of dried grass and store it in the garage until he needed it.

His plan was to go through the entire yard three times, turning the soil each time. Then he'd give the grass a day to dry out in the sun, before raking it out of the way.

If, after the third turn, he couldn't see any more grass or grass roots, he'd call it good and start planting his crops. A third of the yard would be his wheat crop. Another third would be corn, and the rest of the space would be used for a vegetable garden.

He wasn't looking forward to the planting. He knew it would be backbreaking work, and since it was just him now he'd have to work a lot harder to get the crops in. But he'd do it. And he wouldn't complain.

Well, maybe a little bit.

He'd been watching the clouds darken throughout the day, and now as he sniffed the air he could definitely smell rain in the distance.

He smiled, remembering the first time he told Sarah he could smell rain.

She'd said, "Yeah, right!"

Dave just looked at her. He thought everybody could smell rain.

"Seriously."

She was still skeptical.

"You mean to tell me that you can smell rain coming?"

"Yes, of course. I've always been able to. You mean you can't?"

"No. And I think you're pulling my leg, too. What does rain smell like, Mister Smarty Pants?"

Dave was at a loss. How do you describe the smell of rain?

"Gee, I don't know how to describe it, honey. It's sort of like how it smells after a rain, like after the rain cleanses everything. Only not as strong. Like a vague version of that."

She looked at him with her head cocked.

"So, what does your nose tell you exactly, Mr. Prognosticator?"

"Excuse me? We're resorting to name-calling now?"

Sarah laughed the little girl laugh that always won his heart.

"No, silly. A prognosticator is someone who makes predictions. What does your nose tell you? Is it going to rain today?"

"Yes, definitely."

"But it's barely cloudy."

"Doesn't matter. I can smell it in the distance. The smell is being carried in by the same wind that'll bring the rainclouds later today."

"Are you sure you didn't just watch the weather so you could pull a prank on me?"

"Nope. I promise I didn't."

Sarah knew Dave would never break a promise to her, no matter what.

"How sure are you?"

"I'm positive."

"So, if it doesn't rain before nightfall you'll take me out to dinner tomorrow?"

"Sure. But if it does rain before nightfall you have to make me anything I want for dinner tomorrow. Deal?"

"Deal."

"Good. I'll be wanting your world famous lasagna, so you might want to peek into the fridge and make sure we have everything."

"You're pretty sure of yourself, huh?"

"Yep."

At that moment, Sarah's cell phone hand rang. It was her best friend Karen calling.

"Hi, Karen."

"Hi, Sarah. What are you doing?"

"Not much. Just standing in the back yard. Dave is trying to convince me that he can smell rain before it gets here."

"Well, of course he can. I can too. You mean you can't?"

Dave couldn't hear Karen's words, but he could read the expression on Sarah's face and knew pretty much what she'd said.

He laughed and stuck out his tongue.

"Oh, boy. I can't wait for that big ole plate of lasagna…"

He smiled, remembering the conversation as though it had taken place the day before. He could still vividly see the look of disappointment and shock on Sarah's pretty face when she found that others could smell rain and she couldn't.

She later told him she felt deprived.

Then Dave remembered the way Lindsey loved to walk in the summer rain. She'd come to him and take his hand to pull him up from his easy chair.

"Come on, Dad, let's take a walk."

"You nut. It's raining."

"I know. That's why I want to go. That's the best time. The rain washes away all of the ugliness and dirt, and leaves everything refreshed."

"Are you serious?"

"Yes, Dad. Are you getting so old that you've lost the desire to play in the rain?"

And as usual, he gave in to her. He almost always did when his daughters wanted something.

Lindsey was still on his mind as he finished putting the dried grass into the last of the lawn and leaf bags. He was tossing them over the fence from the Hansens' yard into his own when the first drops started to fall.

–29–

As the first drops hit his face, Dave shifted into high gear. He tossed the last of the bags over the fence and then ran back to the Hansen house. He removed the snap-on lids from the Hefty cans at the corners of the house so the runoff from the roof would fill them. Then he scrambled back into his own yard, careful to close his hidden gate behind him. He didn't want any of the rabbits to get into the Hansens' yard and take up residence there.

He grabbed the bags of grass and tossed them onto the back deck. Then he removed the lids from the Hefty cans at the corners of his own house, just as the rainwater began pouring out of the downspouts.

Spring rains in San Antonio came in torrents. He knew it wouldn't take long for all of the cans to fill, and while it wouldn't be suitable for drinking, it would provide him with a lot of water to irrigate his crops with.

He stopped only long enough to catch his breath before going back into the yard. The rabbits were scrambling for shelter under the eaves of the house or on the deck, and probably thought the human insane for going out into the downpour.

But Dave still had a lot of work to do.

He went to the east fence and picked up the tarp that was rolled up against it. He unrolled it, hooking the grommets on one side of the tarp to the screws on the top rail of the fence. The other side was stretched to the two fence posts he'd buried before, and was hooked to screws on top of the posts.

Then he retrieved a Hefty can from the deck and placed in between the posts, at the spot where the center of the tarp dipped down slightly. Immediately, water began flowing into the can.

While the first can was filling, Dave ran to the west side of the yard and did the same thing with his second rain tarp.

He had only a few minutes to catch his breath, and shifted into a lower gear.

The empty water bottles were already close by. He'd taken them from the attic a couple of days before and piled them, still in trash bags, on the back deck. Now he walked over to the deck and started moving them into the yard, next to the Hefty cans.

The cans were rapidly filling with water now. The east can was three quarters of the way full.

Dave ripped open one of the trash bags and took out the first of about twenty empty two liter soda bottles. He removed the cap and shoved it beneath the water, watching the bubbles rise quickly to the surface as it filled with rain water.

He had no time to be neat and organized. He wanted to stay ahead of the rain, so he could fill all of his remaining bottles. And he'd never stopped to count them, but he was certain he had at least two hundred or better.

As each bottle was filled, Dave capped it and tossed it aside haphazardly into the yard. There would be plenty of time later to gather them and store them neatly in the house, out of the view of anyone peeking over the fence.

The rain was coming down in buckets now, and he was barely keeping up. He switched back and forth between the east and west barrels, trying his best to keep them from overflowing, but he was losing the battle.

It was backbreaking work. The full bottles of water weren't heavy, weighing in at only seven pounds apiece. But after filling the first hundred or so, then tightly screwing the lids on before tossing them aside, he began to hurt. His back, his forearms, his hands. Had it really been so long since he'd done so much work that his body was actually rebelling? Was he in such a weakened state that a relatively easy task would wear him down?

He sloughed it off. He'd have time to worry about such things later. Right now he had a battle to fight.

He desperately tried to catch every drop of water, even as the can behind him began to overflow.

Part of him, the little devil that perched upon his shoulder and sometimes got him into trouble, told him to slow down.

"You already have plenty of water," the little devil said. "Between these bottles and the ones you filled from the tap, you'll have five hundred bottles. That's four hundred gallons, more or less. And that will last you a very long time. So relax. Take a break. Sit down and rest for awhile."

But Dave knew better.

He knew that although the rains came frequently and torrentially in the springtime, the summers in San Antonio were a different story altogether. Summers tended to be very dry, sometimes bordering on drought conditions.

He also knew that once he planted his crops, he'd have to irrigate them to keep them alive. And as his rabbit population grew, he'd have to share his water with them as well.

Yes, four hundred gallons packed away in plastic bottles seemed like a lot. And yes, he'd have three hundred more gallons available for the crops in the rain barrels.

But once spring transitioned into summer, he'd use more water than he could replace. And if he didn't get as much as possible stored now, he might pay a heavy price later on.

Dave was disheartened when he looked over at the barrels beneath the rain gutters. Both were overflowing, pouring hundreds of gallons of precious water onto the ground. The barrel behind him was doing the same thing, despite his efforts.

So he did the only thing he could do. He pressed on, and cursed himself for not planning better.

Yes, it was true that if Sarah and the girls had been there, the four of them would likely have been able to keep up.

But it was also true that if Sarah and the girls were there, they would have needed to stockpile even more water. It takes a lot more water to keep four people alive than it does for one.

There had to be a better way. He just had to find it.

–30–

Hi, honey.

I feel like such an idiot. We got our first heavy rainfall yesterday, and I wasn't ready for it.

I thought I was. I had all the barrels in place, and the empty bottles prepositioned on the deck. Still, I couldn't keep up with it all, and so much water slipped through my fingers and rolled away.

I remember a talk we had not long before you guys left for Kansas City. We were sitting on the deck, looking out at the stars, and you asked me if I thought we were ready for the blackout when it came.

I, being my usual macho self, told you we were. I said we'd thought it all through. That we'd left nothing out, and had planned for everything.

Now I realize how stupid I was. And how poorly prepared we were.

First, we had no plan to reconcile if we were far apart when the EMP hit. Yes, we had backpacks full of water and energy bars in each vehicle, and in each of the girls' school lockers in case any of us had to hike across town to get home. Yes, we trained the girls to walk out of school immediately when the EMP hit, and to walk directly home. We taught them to spend the night in abandoned cars if it took more than a day, and not to talk to anyone along the way.

We thought we had it covered. And it never occurred to me, not even in my wildest dreams, that we'd be stuck a thousand miles apart.

If it were only that, I'd accept it as an anomaly. One single oversight in all of our months of planning.

But the water situation showed me that there were other places I've dropped the ball. I should have planned better. I should have been a lot smarter.

I guess I should look at the bright side. I got all the bottles filled. And when I ran out of bottles, I took two large pitchers from the kitchen and made dozens of trips from the rain barrels to the bathtubs. I got both of them filled as well as the kitchen sink and pretty much everything in the house that's capable of holding water.

Right now it's too muddy outside to do much. After the ground dries out in a couple of days I'll plant the corn crop. Then I'll plant the wheat and then the garden vegetables.

My plan is to use the water in the house first for irrigation, then to start emptying all of the barrels. They're all full, but I have nothing to put additional water in. It sucks to admit it, but if we got another good rainstorm tomorrow, it would all go to waste. Every single drop.

I inventoried the soda bottles. There are eight hundred and six of them. That's a little bit of good news, I suppose.

That's far more than I'd have guessed, and I'm amazed that we drank that much soda in two and a half years.

There's got to be a better plan, but I'll be damned if I know what it is. I've been racking my brain to come up with something, but so far I'm running on empty.

By the way, and I have to tell you this because it's so unlike me. When I woke up this morning, I was so sore that I just said to hell with it and rolled over and went back to sleep. I didn't wake up until around noon. I could have slept longer, but I was afraid if I didn't get my lazy ass out of bed I'd stay there all day.

It was downright painful, getting out of bed. I don't know if it was the digging and the raking before the rain, or bending into the barrels filling all of those bottles during the rain. Actually, it could have been the running back and forth between the yard and the bathtubs with the tea pitchers.

Or maybe it was all of it. Whatever the case, I am more sore today than I've ever been in my life.

Anyway, here's the punch line… after I got up, I realized that I didn't really have anything to do. All of my inside projects have been done. I have plenty of things to do outside, but I can't because both of the yards are a muddy mess.

I wound up spending a good portion of the afternoon sitting on the deck, watching the rabbits humping each other in the wet grass. I can almost taste that rabbit steak now.

One thing I did do was try to clean up some of the mud I tracked into the house. If you were here you'd have killed me. I didn't want to waste a lot of water, so I sopped most of the mud up with bath towels. After I got most of it up, I poured just a cup or so of water on the floor and used one last towel to finish the job.

It wouldn't meet your cleanliness standards by a long shot, but I'm a man, and you always said men aren't much different than bears.

The carpet between the back door and the bathrooms is totally shot. It's damp and muddy and I know of no way to clean it. Sorry.

As for the muddy towels, I'll hang them on the clothesline so the next rainfall can wash them for me. The line's full of my underwear and t-shorts now. They got a good washing, and as soon as they're dry I'll bring them in. I'm glad, because I ran out of clean underwear several days ago.

Dirty underwear. Seems like a sad place to end this, but it is what it is. I love you.

–31–

It turned out that the solution to Dave's water collection problem was right under his nose.

On the day after the rain, he sat on his deck, still waiting for the muddy ground to dry out, when it occurred to him that the stench of decaying bodies was gone.

He was convinced that it was a temporary respite. He knew the bodies were still out there, and once they dried from the torrential rains the smells would be back. But the break would be nice while it lasted.

It occurred to him that the rains had come down pretty heavy during the deluge, and his street was on a slight incline. Had the torrent been strong enough to wash the remains of the dead looter down the hill to the storm drain at the end of the street?

He hadn't looked out the front window in several now, and he climbed up the stairs hoping to see the vulture-picked bones washed away.

He wound up being disappointed, and elated, at the same time.

The body was still there. It had shifted position, and had been washed fifty feet or so closer to the bottom of the hill. It was, in fact, directly in front of Dave's house now.

He decided that wasn't necessarily a bad thing. Perhaps any future looters might assume the front of Dave's house was a dangerous place to be and would steer clear of it.

But that wasn't what made him elated.

What made him elated was the site of a long line of garbage cans, sitting on the street, and as far as the eyes could see.

He'd forgotten that the day the EMP hit, two months before, had been garbage day.

He kicked himself for being so stupid. The answer was there, in the street right below his window, the whole time.

He'd been so confident that his well made plans would provide plenty of water for a family of four. But he watched thousands of gallons slip from his grasp and fall to the ground. Even if his family had been there to help him, it wouldn't have mattered. They'd still have run out of vessels to put the water in.

If only he'd had thought ahead of time. If only he'd have retrieved some of those cans. He could have filled every one of them with water as well.

Dave suddenly had a new mission. One he could do while he was waiting for the ground to dry. One that would prevent the same thing from happening again the next time it rained.

Something that could expand his water stores exponentially.

Something that theoretically could save his life someday.

The EMP had hit that day before the garbage truck had come down the street. Nearly all of the cans were still filled with a mixture of garbage and rainwater, except for a couple that had been turned over by dogs looking for food.

They would be heavy because of the water weight. They'd make a lot of noise if he just pushed them over. He'd have to tip them over quietly and let the water drain from them, then slide the trash out of them and onto the street. It was risky. He might come across a trigger-happy neighbor who'd mistake him for a looter.

But he had no choice. It was an opportunity he just couldn't pass up.

He had one thing on his side that gave him an advantage over his neighbors, and anyone else who might be about.

Dave could see in the dark.

Not literally, of course. But with the aid of the night vision goggles he'd packed away in his Faraday cage, he could see several hundred yards in almost total darkness. It would be a great tool to use for this project.

At just after midnight, Dave unlocked the bar that held his garage door down, and very slowly eased it up about a foot and a half. He did so with some apprehension, because he knew it was prone to squeaking. But he got lucky this time, and it didn't make a sound. He took that as a good omen.

He lay down next to the door and rolled out into the driveway. Then he came to one knee, very slowly, and looked both ways, up and down the street.

He did everything deliberately slowly, because he knew that in the darkness, fast movements could catch the eye of someone watching and give him away.

Still from a kneeling position, he pulled his AR-15 rifle from the garage and carefully lowered the door.

It was a moonless sky. Another good omen. Moonlight was something he didn't need. But it would have made it much easier for others to see him. The stars in the sky gave his night vision goggles plenty of light to amplify into an eerie green field of vision. He couldn't see as well as he'd be able to in the daytime, but he could see far better than anyone else out there.

Carefully, over the next hour, he went from car to shrub to wall, wherever he could find a hiding place, so that he could move up the street in short bursts.

Along the way up one side of the street and down the other, he turned over a total of twenty two garbage cans, slowly and deliberately.

He skipped a few. The tell-tale streams of water coming from the bottoms of some cans indicated they'd been dragged to and from the street so many times that they had cracks or holes in the bottoms. Those were no use to him, so he left them behind.

So far, so good. He made a second loop, once all the cans had been drained of their water, and carefully slid each of the cans out from underneath their garbage. Then he took the cans, two at a time, back to his front yard, and over to the side of his fence.

By three thirty, he'd retrieved all of them.

Now was the tricky part. It was very likely that throwing the cans over the fence would make considerable noise. Certainly enough to wake up curious neighbors and make them look out their windows.

He didn't know if any of the neighbors would be able to make him out in the darkness, in the shadows between his house and the one next door. He certainly didn't want to be mistaken for a prowler and shot at.

He stood back, scratched his head, and came up with a solution.

At least he hoped he did. In theory it would work. But Dave had found in years past that the best laid plans sometimes went awry. So he'd hope for the best.

He laid the first two cans down and inserted one within the other. They were different sizes and shapes, made by different manufacturers, so they didn't fit together well. The second one stuck out about a foot from the top of the first.

But that was okay. That's what he expected and in fact was banking on.

He then put the third can inside the first two, and so on until he had one long stack of trash cans, laying on its side.

So far, so good.

The monstrosity was probably eighteen feet long, but was relatively light. So light, in fact, that Dave could start at one end, lift it up, and then walk beneath it, lifting it higher and higher as he went.

Until the stack was upright and leaning against his fence.

Then he grabbed the bottom of the stack and lifted it up, until the weight of the top-heavy stack caused it to tip silently over the fence and come to rest on the other side, in his back yard.

He paused for a full minute, watching in both directions up and down the street for any sign of movement. Then he made his way back to his overhead garage door, eased it up, and rolled back inside.

After securing the garage, he went into the back yard and carefully eased the tall stack of trash cans to the ground. And one by one he slid them from the stack and carried them to his back yard, out of view of anyone peeking over his fence.

–32–

Dave stood on a ladder late the next afternoon, after he'd slept most of the day. It was hard cutting into the aluminum gutter from above, at an awkward angle. It was made even harder because he was trying to do so quietly. He had an insanc vision in his head of a man in prison, using a smuggled file, to quietly saw at the bars of his cell while everyone slept around him.

It took him almost an hour to cut the first notch in the bottom of the gutter. It was about the size of a quarter, and during a heavy rainstorm would provide a good-sized stream of water to flow into the trash can below.

He moved three feet to the left, and started the next notch.

His arms were burning by this time, mostly because to cut the notches in the gutter he had to reach the saw up and saw downward. But he'd fight through the pain. He didn't want to give in to a little bit of pain and then end up cursing himself again if the rains came back before he was ready.

By nightfall, he quit simply because he couldn't raise his arm anymore.

He finished the first four of the notches, and had four of the trash cans lined up in a neat little row beneath them, each ready to catch their fill of rainwater.

It was a good start.

The following morning the ground was finally dry enough to start planting his crops. He knew it would take longest for the corn to grow to maturity, so he'd plant the corn crop first. Then the wheat, then everything else.

The corn was going to be a pain in the ass. He knew that going in. But it had to be done.

The privacy fence in the back yard of the Hansen house was eight feet tall – two feet higher than his own.

He was fairly confident that none of the corn would grow that tall, but he started the first row three feet inside the fence line, just in case.

The ground was barren now, free of grass and weeds. It was no longer mud, but rather soft packed dirt. His feet left slight depressions, which gave him a great idea.

In the back of the garage were a couple of extra fence posts. He didn't need them for the outhouse or rain tarp projects. He'd just bought them in case he dreamed up a use for them later on.

He told Sarah at the time, "If we ever need them for a new project, they'll be here. If we don't need them, we can burn them for fuel at some point. One way or the other they'll get used."

For now, though, he had a perfect use for one of them.

He put on a pair of heavy leather work gloves. The project would require a lot of manhandling of the post, and he didn't relish the idea of ending his day with hands full of blisters and wood splinters. Hopefully, the gloves would prevent both.

Back in the Hansen yard, he found the spot where he planned to plant the first of many corn seeds, lifted up the post, and pounded it into the ground.

It left a depression about an inch deep. A perfect little four inch square hole that would retain the precious water Dave poured for the seed every couple of days, without letting it roll away and go to waste.

Dave worked backwards, so he could see the depressions he'd already made. By doing so he was able to make the first row fairly straight and evenly spaced.

He took a short break and counted the depressions. There were sixty of them.

As he caught his breath, he did the math. Sixty plants per row, and he figured maybe twelve rows. He had no clue how many ears of corn each stalk would yield, but he knew he'd have an awful lot of corn when it came time to harvest it.

The wheat would go right next to the corn, to the west. He planned to plant thirty rows of wheat too, but the plants would be a lot closer together.

On the other side of the wheat, he'd plant a regular vegetable garden. Tomatoes and squash and cucumbers and a dozen other vegetables. Each would require individual watering, plant by plant. After all the seeds were planted he expected to work pretty much from dawn to dusk, every day.

But he had nothing better to do.

–33–

Hi Sarah.

I hope you and the girls are doing well. I've been totally miserable the last few days, missing you. I've decided it's the little things I miss the most. Listening to you breathe at night when I can't sleep. Watching the morning sun against your face when I wake up before you on a Saturday morning. Holding your hand in the supermarket.

I miss you so much.

I don't remember if I told you, but I've been sleeping on your pillow for the last couple of weeks. It gave me comfort, because it smelled like your hair. When I closed my eyes I could almost pretend you were there, laying beside me where you belong. I think it made me sleep better.

The scent is starting to fade now, or I've gotten used to it. In either case, I don't notice it when I lay down anymore. I have to bury my face deep into the pillow to find it again. I hope it never goes away completely. It would be like losing you all over again.

I've spent the last three days going back and forth between the Hansen house and our own yard. Planting the seeds is back breaking work. I made depressions where I want each seed to go, to retain water later on. It helps me keep the rows straight, but planting the seeds themselves is still a pain in the butt. I'm having to crawl on my hands and knees from one depression to the next.

We never discussed the method we'd use to plant the crops. I guess we probably should have. But I always took it for granted that you'd be here when it came time for that, and that you'd lead the way.

I hope I'm doing it right, without you here to guide me. The method I've chosen to use it to poke a hole in the ground in the middle of each of my depressions. I'm poking it about an inch deep, dropping in a seed, and then using my thumb to press down on the soft dirt to cover it. Whenever I finish a row, I carry pitchers of water from the bathtub, and pour about a cup or so into each depression.

Do you think that's enough? I sure wish you were here to guide me. You've always been the gardener in the family. I've always sucked at it.

Anyway, I don't want to overwater the crops and waste any of the water. I figured I'd start out with a cup every day until they came up, and then look at the leaves. If they look dry, like they need more, I'll increase their water. If the leaves are soft and green I'll keep it at a cup per day.

I'm already tired of lugging the water back and forth. I could use the rain barrels at the Hansen house, but I want to get the water out of the house first. It's grown stagnant and is starting to smell up the place. Once the tubs and sinks are empty, I'll start using the barrel water.

I'm also still sawing notches in the rain gutters for the additional trash cans I took from the street. I'm going back and forth. When the planting makes my back and knees hurt to the point where I desperately need a break, I switch off for awhile and cut the notches. Then when cutting the notches wears out my arm to the point where I can't lift it any more, I go back to planting.

I have four notches left to cut, and should finish them tonight. I should finish planting the corn tomorrow, and will start the wheat after that.

I wish you were here to help. Shoot, I wish you were here for a million different reasons.

Mostly because I need you by my side. That's where you belong. Not a thousand damn miles away.

–34–

By the time Dave finished the fifth row of wheat, he desperately needed a break from planting seeds. He'd finished the notches a couple of days before, which was great. But without that occasional respite from the crop, he'd been planting full time. And his back hurt so bad he could barely walk.

So it was actually pretty good timing that he happened to run low on drinking water that very same day.

He and Sarah had stockpiled twenty cases of bottled drinking water. Their thinking was that if the EMP occurred during the summer time, when rainfalls were few and far between, and if they weren't able to get any backup from the tap, that the drinking water would get them by until the next rainfall.

Dave had been careful to save all of the empty bottles, and now that he was down to the last case, he knew it was time to refill them.

His plan was simple. He'd use the camp stove and disposable bottles of propane to bring the rainwater to a boil for ten minutes. Then he'd let it cool, while a second stew pot heated up and boiled. Then a third.

He figured that by the time the third pot boiled for ten minutes, the first pot would be cool enough to pour into the bottles. Then he could refill the first pot with more rainwater and continue the cycle.

While he sat on the deck, watching the first pot come to a slow boil, he nursed his aching muscles. He never knew that farming could be this hard. He had a new respect for farmers. Although they had fancy equipment to help them along that he didn't have, he felt somewhat of a kinship with them. He knew that they, too, worked from dawn to dusk and went to bed each night with their muscles and joints crying out in pain.

And he wondered if it got easier in time.

He looked at his watch. The water had been boiling for three minutes now. Seven more to go.

And it was while he was waiting those other seven minutes that he decided to pay a visit to the house next door.

The family that had lived there had seemed nice enough. Sarah and Dave had been careful not to allow themselves to get too close to any of the neighbors. They knew the solar storms were coming, and didn't want to feel any guilt when they holed themselves up and left the neighbors to fend for themselves.

But the Castro family always seemed to have smiles on their faces, and always waved to Dave and Sarah when they found themselves outside at the same time.

For a moment Dave wondered if he should have done something to help the Castros after the blackout. Perhaps given them some of his water. Or shared some of his knowledge.

Then he decided, no. The whole world had the chance to prepare just as he and Sarah had. The signs were all over the place. All of the cable channels had been running shows about a coming apocalypse. The news ran stories daily about how the earth was warming, and predicted bad things ahead.

Anyone who didn't prepare to at least some degree was foolish.

Dave felt bad for caring so little about a nice family. And he wished them well and would continue to pray for them when he did his nightly prayers. But in the end, he owed them nothing more than that.

And he knew that wherever they'd gone, they would be doing whatever they needed to do to survive, just like the rest of the world was doing. If they needed food, or water, or shelter, they'd beg for it, or barter whatever they had. And if they had nothing, they'd find houses to break into. Because that's the type of world they all lived in now.

And it was that knowledge that drove Dave, without apprehension or remorse, to decide to break into the Castro home and take whatever he could use.

It had been weeks now since he saw them walk away, and he knew they hadn't returned.

He had no idea where they went or why. Probably to the home of a relative they knew was better prepared than they were. He hoped they made it there safely and were still alive. But whether they were alive or not, he was fairly confident they wouldn't be back.

He went to the garage and retrieved his keyhole saw.

Then, after checking his boiling water, he went to the fence on the east side of his yard and made the first cut.

–35–

After the third cut, He went back into the garage to get several sliding bolts, and paused long enough to take the second pot of rainwater off the fire. He put the third pot on, and would come back in a few minutes to check on its progress.

Twenty minutes later, with the second pot of water boiling vigorously, Dave finished the project. The hidden gate was the same size as the one leading into the Hansen yard, and would give him ready access to the house next door anytime he needed it.

He checked his watch. The first pot had been cooling for about fifty minutes now. He wondered if that was enough.

He stuck his finger into the first pot of water. It was still pretty warm, taking longer than he expected to cool off. He might have to turn the burner off after the fourth pot, and take a break. He was afraid that if he poured water into the bottles while it was too hot, it might leech too many chemicals from the plastic and become a health risk.

Then he laughed out loud at his own stupidity. Here he was, seemingly alone in the world, surrounded by hundreds, maybe thousands of dead bodies, and hearing gunshots near and far each and every night.

And he was worried about getting cancer someday.

He took the first empty water bottle and placed a small yellow funnel into its top. Then he very slowly and carefully lifted the pot and poured a small stream of water into the funnel.

He was cautious not to spill any of the liquid, which he realized was more precious now than gold.

Each bottle got a bit easier to fill, as he got better with the process and the heavy stew pot got lighter. When he filled the last bottle, he took a count. Seventeen bottles of water. Enough for two to three days, more or less. He'd hoped there would be more than that. But by the end of the day, he wouldn't have any problems filling enough bottles to last him a month or more.

And he'd better get used to the process. This would likely be a regular chore that he'd have to perform for the rest of his life.

He filled the first stew pot back up and put it back on the fire. While it was heating, he'd sneak next door and check out the Castro place.

There were two curious rabbits nearby as he unbolted the section of fence and prepared to set it aside. He shooed them away, so they wouldn't follow him into the neighbor's yard and have to be chased down.

Once on the other side, he took another slide bolt and a Phillips screwdriver from his pocket. He held the fence section in place with one hand while he pressed the small screws into the soft fir of the fence slats.

He'd only need one bolt on this side. It wasn't meant to secure the fence. Its sole purpose was to keep the section from falling back into Dave's yard while he was in the Castro house, and letting all the rabbits out.

Once the fence section was bolted into place, Dave went to the sliding back door.

He was almost positive that the house was empty, but he knocked anyway. He didn't know why, exactly. An old habit, maybe.

Or maybe it just wasn't right to enter another family's home without announcing yourself. Even if you knew the family was long gone.

He tried the sliding door, also out of habit, although he didn't really expect it to be unlocked.

But it was.

And since it was, he was now suspicious that looters had either been here and gone, or were still here.

He took his 9 mm handgun from its holster and very slowly slid the door open.

He'd already announced his presence when he knocked. If anyone was inside, they had two choices. They could confront him, or they could go out the front door.

He slid the door closed behind him.

He spoke in a loud, firm voice. "I mean you no harm. I'm only here for supplies. I am armed and will defend myself, but I'd rather just look around and go in peace."

There was no answer.

He went cautiously from room to room on the lower floor. Then he crept up the stairs and went from room to room.

Once he was convinced the house was empty, he returned to the first floor and looked around a bit more thoroughly.

The front door was also unlocked. He found that doubly odd.

The house was immaculate, which led him to believe that looters hadn't been there. He had no way of knowing for sure, but he guessed that when looters went through a house they weren't very neat about the way they searched for things. And in this house, nothing looked out of place.

He went to the kitchen, and wasn't surprised to see that most of the food was gone. There was no water at all, which also didn't surprise him.

On the dining room table he found a handwritten note, which seemed to explain it all.

With heavy heart, we are leaving our home, and do not expect to return. We have gone to live with friends. They are what we once called "preppers." We used to tease them. We used to say they were wasting their time. Now it appears they were smarter than all of us. And thankfully they're good people, for despite our teasing they have asked us to join them.

We leave behind everything except a few clothes and family heirlooms. It no longer seems to have the value it once did. Feel free to make use of whatever you need. It's no longer doing us any good.

May God have mercy on us all.

Jack and Eva Castro

Dave was suddenly sad that he hadn't gotten to know this family better. They must have been good people, to donate their possessions to others so willingly.

He was glad that they had a safe place to go, and hoped that they would survive.

–36–

Hi, honey.

It's been a long day, but I got several things accomplished.

You always said I couldn't boil water, but today I proved you wrong. I boiled a total of nine pots of water, and filled up enough water bottles to keep me going for at least a month.

Let me tell you, I dreaded that first drink of rain water. I thought that even after boiling, it would taste nasty. But I was pleasantly surprised. It actually tasted better than the tap water did before the blackout. I suppose because it doesn't have the fluoride or other chemicals. I'm a fan already.

I also finally went over to the Castros' house. They left a note behind when they bugged out and invited whoever dropped in to help themselves. They even left both doors unlocked. They said they had a safe place to go to ride out the crisis, with some friends of theirs who are preppers.

I wish we'd have gotten to know them better. If they ever come back, I think I'd like to. They seem, in hindsight, as nice people.

They didn't have much food left over there. A few bags of dried beans, Ramen noodles, and lasagna noodles. Things that require water to cook. There wasn't a drop of water in the whole place. I think they only left the food behind because they thought it was worthless if they couldn't cook it. They could have eaten it dry, instead of letting it go to waste. But then they'd have been thirstier, and maybe they were just too low on water to do that.

In any event, I spent an hour or so going through the place, gathering up what I could use. Guess what! They were apparently recyclers. In the garage I found a couple of large plastic bags full of aluminum can, which I left behind. But I also found three bags full of empty soda, water and milk jugs. I didn't count them, but I'm guessing as many as a hundred more.

I also grabbed all of the pitchers and pots from their kitchen, and the trash cans, hardware and tools from their garage. Lastly, I cleaned them out of toilet paper, got some books and magazines to help pass my time, and a boatload of candles. It appeared they were a very religious family. Most of the candles were the type that Catholic families burn, with pictures of saints and stuff on them. I hope I don't go to hell for taking them, but I figure I might as well make use of them.

While I was in their garage, I found an old piece of rain gutter leaning up against the wall in the corner. Sure enough, I pulled aside the curtain in their front room and peeked out, and they do indeed have a gutter system that runs along the front of their house.

It's funny how you never notice such things.

Anyway, I'm going to see if there's a moon out tonight. If there isn't, and if it's cloudy or overcast, I'm going to haul my ladder over there and see how hard it would be to take the gutter down. I already examined the fascia and sub fascia on the back side of the house. The wood is old, and rather soft. I shouldn't have any trouble forcing screws into it, even without a drill. It sure would be nice to be able to get the storm runoff from their house as well.

I have the corn crop planted, and I've started the wheat crop. I've been thinking, and I don't like the idea of leaving a work row between rows of plants. I know I have to get in there to water them, but it seems like such a waste of space.

Since you weren't here, I tried something different on my own. I hope it works. When I planted the wheat, I planted the second row just ten inches from the first one, but the seeds are staggered. Then I did a work row and planted two rows of wheat on the other side. I made them staggered so I could still reach every plant when I went through to water them, but that way I only needed one work row for four rows of wheat instead of two.

My only concern is whether or not planting them so close together will affect their yield. If the yield is poor, I'll know better next time.

Thumper is looking at me as I'm writing this. I'm not sure what he wants. I talk to him sometimes when I'm out back working. Maybe he wants to ask my advice about something.

I hope he doesn't want any advice about sex. He's been doing much better than me in that department lately. In fact, both of the females are very big now. I don't know how long it takes to make rabbit babies, but I'm guessing we'll have a lot of little rabbits very soon.

Tell the girls not to worry. I haven't forgotten my promise not to kill their pets. I'll let them live to be a ripe old age and die on their own. I'll settle for eating their offspring instead. When Thumper and the other old timers die on their own, I'll bury them in the back yard with a proper funeral.

I hope you're back by then. I have a huge hole in my heart that only the three of you can fill.

Kiss the girls for me. I love you, sweetheart. I wish I knew if you were ever going to read my words...

–37–

Once again, Dave found himself out in the open in the cover of darkness. This time he was on a ladder, in front of the Castro house, carefully taking down their gutter system.

It was a slow process. The night vision goggles allowed him to see each of the screws holding the gutter in place. But the green glow they provided didn't make out the fine details he needed to see the screw head. He had to hold the screwdriver tip against the screw with one hand while he turned it with the other. All while balancing on an uneven ladder.

At one point he had to take a break and scramble down the ladder when he heard voices coming from the end of the block. He folded the ladder and laid it in the tall grass of the front yard, then scampered into the bushes.

He drew his sidearm, hoping he wouldn't be outgunned. And he computed his chances of making it back into his garage unseen.

He looked in the direction of the voices and could make out three shadowy figures, walking down the center of the street. Two of them carried rifles, although the green haze of the goggles prevented him from telling what type.

They were now only three houses away. He had no chance of making it back into his garage.

It struck him that this was the most vulnerable he'd been since the crisis began.

It also struck him that he was not afraid.

He wondered why. Any man with any sense would be afraid, or at least nervous, at the prospect of dying. But he felt nothing other than curiosity. Curiosity about the men walking up the street. Who they were, what they were up to. And where they were going.

He held his position, zeroing in on one of the two men with rifles. At the first sign of trouble, he'd be the first to go. Then the one with the other rifle. The man with the hand gun would be the least threat, and would therefore be the last to die.

But the men never noticed him kneeling behind the bushes. They passed him by and continued on their way, up the street, their voices getting harder to hear with each step they took.

Dave took up a new position behind Jack Castro's car, which was parked in the driveway when the EMP hit. He watched the three as they completely disappeared from view.

And he reflected on what happened.

He could easily have died, yet he felt no fear. Did that mean he no longer cared whether he lived or died?

Did that mean he'd given up?

Then he realized he was more interested in hearing the men's words, to hear what they were talking about, than he was about the prospect of getting shot.

Was he so starved for human contact that he would ignore obvious danger to expose himself to others, at his own peril?

And if that's what had happened, if he was so starved for human interaction that he'd risk his own life to see it, how far was he from total madness?

He finally decided he was not going mad. That he was stuck in the bushes through circumstance and for no other reason. That he did indeed have no other option, and didn't have enough time to return to the safety of his garage.

Further, he decided that he wasn't desperate to hear their words. He was merely curious, after having no other contact with any human being for many weeks.

Lastly, he decided that he had no fear because he knew he had the upper hand in the situation. He could see without being seen. The flash from his first shot would give away his position, sure. But it wouldn't have given his adversaries time to react.

Dave was an excellent shot. He could fire off three shots in as many seconds, and was fairly confident of three hits. Maybe not kill shots, but all three of his targets would go down. The next few shots would finish them off.

He finally decided that he was no more afraid now than he was on patrol, with the U.S. Marines in Fallujah. Just like in Iraq, he was on the good side. They had the firepower, and the weapons, and the training and tactics to get the job done. The only thing the enemy had was the element of surprise. And surprise was way overrated when matched against vastly superior firepower.

Even though he'd been outnumbered three to one, Dave was confident he would have been the victor. That's why he wasn't afraid.

Fear is for suckers.

–38–

It took Dave another hour to get the gutter pieces off the front of the house. He carried them over to his own yard and slid them one at a time over his fence, careful to avoid the painful screws on top of the fence slats.

He checked his watch. It was a little after three a.m.

He figured he was out in the open anyway. He might as well do some more work while he was here.

Much as he'd done a few nights before, he stealthily made his way down the street, quietly turning over trash cans. He was careful to lay them down gently, instead of just pushing them over.

After he'd toppled ten cans there were no more to topple. The piles of trash he could see down the rest of the block told him that someone else had the same idea he did.

He wished them well. Ten additional cans was all he needed to line the entire back side of the house next door.

He crouched behind a car and waited a few minutes to see if his activity had brought anyone outside of their homes.

While he waited Dave pondered how difficult it must be for a looter to determine which houses were still occupied. Since the crisis began, the Castros weren't the only family he saw walk away from their homes in search of help or a better situation. He'd seen a dozen other families do the same. Sometimes in the night, and sometimes in broad daylight.

He suspected that many, if not most, of these houses were now vacant. And since the almost overwhelming stench of decaying flesh had returned not long after the rainfall, he also suspected that many of them contained the bodies of suicide victims. He suspected that many held entire families, who'd chosen the easy way out instead of fighting for survival.

The looters must be having a dreadful time, he reasoned, in determining which houses to break into. It wasn't just a matter of seeing which houses had no lights or activity. None of them did. Peeking in the windows at night did no good, since they couldn't see anything.

For the looters, it was a deadly game of chance. They were breaking into houses hoping they were empty. But if they weren't, they might be confronted by angry homeowners and end up like the hapless thief lying in front of Dave's house.

Dave wondered how many of the gunshots he heard at night were homeowners protecting their property.

Or maybe armed looters blowing away unarmed and innocent people to make it easier to steal whatever they had.

Dave was glad of two things. He was glad that he'd taken the time and effort to make his home appear to be vacant. Thus far, it had apparently worked. Besides the two occasions when he'd actually seen strangers trying to make out his signs in the dark, no one had ever tried to break in, or even to knock on the door.

The other thing he was glad for was that he was well armed. Even before the EMP hit, he was a big supporter of the second amendment. Sarah was too, but only in a practical sense. She didn't like firing guns. She said they were heavy and she lacked the arm strength to control the kick of the larger handguns. But she realized they would be an essential tool to survive in a post-apocalyptic world. So she tried to like them, bless her heart. She went to the range occasionally, and fired often enough to stay proficient.

She always said she would only fire a weapon to protect her family, but that was good enough for Dave. He said that was the only time he planned to use his as well.

"We're not robbers or thieves," he told her. "We're the good guys. But if the good guys aren't armed and willing to defend themselves, the bad guys will take over the world. Because you can damn sure bet the bad guys will have guns."

After several minutes he decided it was quiet enough to proceed. He gathered the cans, two at a time, and ferried them to the fence at the side of his house. Then, as he'd done before, he formed them into a stack and carefully flipped the stack over the fence.

Then he retrieved his ladder, slowly slid it beneath his overhead garage door, and followed it into the garage.

The last two things he did on this night was move the pieces of rain gutter and trash cans into the center of his back yard, and then go to bed exhausted.

–39–

As he'd done the previous time he'd worked long into the night, Dave slept well past noon.

He struggled to remember a dream he'd had, but he could only recall bits and pieces. Two men, who had somehow discovered that Dave was living there. They'd broken in while Dave was sleeping and surprised him. There was a brief skirmish. Dave shot one of the men dead, and found himself in his back yard, out of ammunition for his handgun and unable to get to either of his AR-15s.

Although he couldn't remember the whole dream, it troubled him greatly.

It reminded him that he still hadn't prepared his bug out location.

In the months leading up to the solar storm that sent the EMP, or multiple EMPs, raining down on the earth, Dave and Sarah had prepared the arsenal they'd need to survive an assault.

They'd purchased two AR-15 rifles, two 9 millimeter pistols, and several hundred rounds of ammo for each.

Now Dave was on his own, and suddenly had two extra weapons on his hands.

He'd known for quite some time that he needed a backup plan in case he was overrun. He just hadn't acted on it. There was always something else that needed to be done.

His dream reminded him that putting it off any longer was dangerous. And, in fact, he was damn lucky it hadn't already happened.

He always had his handgun on his hip. He always had his AR-15 close by. Even on the occasions he had gone outside his sanctuary and onto the street, it was laying on his garage floor, just inside the overhead door, where he could have reached it if he'd needed it.

But he could only shoot one rifle at a time. The second one would be better left at his bug out location, in the event he had to evacuate his home and leave his primary weapon behind.

It was an ugly thought. But in a survival situation, the people most likely to go on living are the ones who plan for the worst case scenarios.

It was mid afternoon now. He was going to water the crops today, but it was cool and overcast. They'd wait another day.

This mission was more important.

Dave went to the back fence that separated his yard from the Hansen house. It took him two trips to take everything he needed. He lugged a large duffle bag, a back pack, and Sarah's rifle. And a small folding step ladder that Sarah used for reaching the top shelves in the kitchen.

He shooed the rabbits away and removed the secret panel that served as his gateway to the yard behind him. Then he put both bags and the rifle through the fence and followed them, reattaching the fence panel so the rabbits didn't follow.

The back door of the Hansen house had a multi-paned window, and he broke out the small pane of glass closest to the doorknob.

With a hand covered with a heavy leather work glove, he carefully picked out all the jagged edges of glass still stuck in the window's frame. Then he reached his arm in, unlocked the deadbolt and the doorknob, and walked into the house.

He knew the house was completely empty, and that hiding things would be a challenge. There would be no couch he could hide the rifle behind. No box springs to shove bottles of water into. No dresser drawers to hide extra ammo.

Nothing.

But what the house did have was a central heating and air conditioning unit.

And a central heating and air conditioning unit used a series of ducts to move air throughout the house.

Dave guessed that any looters who might break into the Hansen home would immediately see that it was vacant and then leave again.

And even if they stayed awhile, he guessed that they wouldn't reach behind the central air unit to see if there was a rifle hidden there.

And they likely wouldn't unscrew the vent covers from the ceiling and reach inside the ductwork to see if anything was hidden there either.

Dave chuckled. Even if they had a mind to, they wouldn't have been able to reach the vent covers.

But Dave could, with the aid of the step ladder.

The Hansen house was two stories, like his own. From the rear upstairs bedroom of the house, he had a fairly good view of the back of his own house. Good enough, anyway, to get a bead on anyone coming out of the house and into his back yard.

This would be his go-to place if he ever had to evacuate.

He went into the upstairs hallway first and found the central air closet. As he suspected, it was dusty and dirty and obviously hadn't been opened in quite some time.

He'd already taped over the muzzle and closed the ejection port of the weapon to keep out dust and insects. He hid the rifle behind the unit, then stood back to make sure that no parts of it were visible.

Then he turned the thumbscrews that held the front cover of the unit into place. Inside the unit he hid two loaded magazines and three boxes of .556 ammunition.

He replaced the cover, closed the closet door, and went back downstairs.

In the dining room, he removed the vent cover and placed two soda bottles containing the water he'd gotten from the kitchen sink before the tap ran dry. He'd already poured one third of the water into another vessel, so that each bottle was only two thirds full.

That was so the bottles wouldn't burst in the winter time when the water froze into ice and expanded.

He replaced the vent cover and placed two more bottles of water in a kitchen vent twelve feet away.

Into two vents in the living room he placed more water, as well as several Tupperware containers of trail mix. The trail mix would last practically forever, and would sustain him for at least a week, as long as he had water to wash it down with.

Lastly, inside the vent in the den, he placed four boxes of 9 mm bullets, and an extra magazine.

Then he carried the step ladder back up the stairs, pulled down the drop down ladder to the attic, and hid the step ladder beneath the attic insulation.

His bug out site was ready.

If he was ever forced to leave his home, it would be just a temporary measure. He'd come here and sit in his perch in the upstairs bedroom, hoping to get a clear shot at the people who occupied his home. If he couldn't, he'd sit here for a few days until things cooled off, and then storm his home to take it back again.

But he hoped he never had to do that.

-40-

Hi, Sarah.

I hope you and the girls are well.

Today I did one of the most disgusting things I've had to do since the blackout.

I've been trying to find places to hide as much of the bottled water as I can. I've moved most of it up to the attic and hidden it under the blown-in insulation. I've been careful to place the bottles over the joists so they don't crash through the ceiling, and I could only put so much up there.

Then I hid some in each of the ventilation ducts and air returns. You never realize how many of them are in your house until you have to remove the plates, one at a time. There were twenty seven of them, total. I put four bottles into each of them and got rid of over a hundred more bottles.

In the garage I lined up four rows against the east wall, probably eighty bottles total, and then leaned a sheet of plywood against the wall in front of them. Then, on each end of the plywood I stacked a whole bunch of tool boxes and other junk.

Speaking of junk, remember all those cardboard boxes full of books and knick-knacks and blankets and stuff in the garage? Well, they're now full of bottles of water. The stuff that was in the boxes is strewn about all over the garage. The garage is now a colossal mess, but at least the water is well hidden.

I took that huge mattress off of our bed. You know, the one that's like three feet tall, that you had to climb up into every night?

Yeah, that one. I took it off and hollowed it out. When you walk into our bedroom it looks like a normal bed. But when you lift up the mattress you can see that it's actually just a shell now, and covers up forty eight bottles of water.

Man, that mattress held a lot of stuffing. I put it in a big pile on the floor in Lindsey's room. Her room is directly over the safe room. In fact, I have plans to pull a bunch of insulation from the attic and add to the pile. My goal is to make her room knee deep in insulation. That way the safe room will be toasty warm this winter when I crank up the fireplace.

Anyway, back to the disgusting part.

When I was at the Castro house next door, I opened up their chest freezer and found the most disgusting assortment of former food you've ever seen. It all went bad when the power went out. It was green with mold and stunk almost as bad as the decaying bodies outside.

Anyway, long story short, I went back over and dragged all of it over here, in a couple of large trash bags. It almost turned my stomach. But now, it's in our own chest freezer. Any looter who opens our freezer door will see it and smell it and will quickly close the door again. He'll never know that underneath it are fifty five two-liter bottles of drinking water.

So here's the deal. I got all of it hidden except for three bottles. Those three bottles will sit on a shelf, untouched, along with half a box of spaghetti, half a jar of grape jelly, and three packages of ramen noodles.

If anybody ever breaks into the house, I will try my best to convince them that's all I have. I'll tell them that I do the same thing they do. That I go out at night and break into houses and grab whatever food and water I can find.

Hopefully they'll buy it and take what's in the cupboard and leave.

In the meanwhile, my real source of food and water will be the little places all over the house where I've got it hidden.

If that's not good enough, and they want to get ugly, I've got other things hidden around the house as well. Knives, several of them, hidden behind doors and inside pillows. Underneath the center cushion on the couch is your handgun. Just in case mine jams or I ever need a second one.

I hope you don't mind, honey, but I've turned our home into a fortress. But it's a place where I can be confident now that I can survive in. That we can all survive in.

Because I fully expect to find you and the girls, and to bring you all back here some day.

You can take that to the bank.

–41–

Dave had finished his writing and put his log book away before he realized he'd forgotten to tell Sarah the good news. It was the only good news he'd had in awhile, and he'd been just itching to tell her, then he forgot all about it.

But that was okay. He'd write her again in a few days, and she'd hear all about the backyard full of baby rabbits.

The two females had given birth within two days of each other. A couple of them were stillborn, and Dave buried them in the garden at the Hansen house. The rest of them seemed healthy, though. He counted eighteen, between the two litters.

He had no idea how soon the new rabbits would be old enough to breed on their own. If they got to the point where they were breeding so fast he couldn't feed them, he might have to start culling the litters. For now, though, he didn't see any reason he couldn't keep up with them. He loved the taste of rabbit, after all, and he didn't mind the thought of eating it for supper every night for weeks on end.

All in all, the prospect of having too much meat beat the hell out of the alternative of not having enough.

Dave was suddenly startled by the sound of a gunshot. He immediately drew his own weapon and ran up the stairs.

The shot was close. Closer than any of the shots he'd heard in the past. And this one was in broad daylight.

There was something else about this shot, too. As close as it was, it was somehow muffled. It came from the west side of his house. Dave was almost certain it came from the house next door.

The next shot confirmed his suspicions. Again, it was muffled and sounded like it came from within a structure. And again, it was just to the west of Dave's house.

Dave walked back down the stairs and ducked into the safe room. He was certain now that no one was shooting at him. But if bullets were flying in the house next door, there was a possibility that a stray bullet might find its way into his house. The only safe place to be was within the safe room with its bulletproof walls.

As he walked into the safe room, a third shot rang out.

He and Sarah didn't know the people next door at all. The family had only moved in a couple of months before the blackout.

In fact, he'd only seen the man one time.

About a month before the blackout, he'd come knocking on Dave's front door. Dave remembered opening the door with some apprehension, thinking it was a salesman. Or even worse, a Jehovah's witness.

"Hi," the tall, red-headed man said. "Is there a Sarah Anna Speer that lives here?"

Dave replied, "Uh, yes…"

The man produced a woman's magazine.

"This is for her. The mailman left it in my box by mistake."

Dave smiled and took the magazine. They introduced themselves, although for the life of him Dave couldn't remember the man's name.

A fourth shot rang out.

Dave recalled mentioning the encounter at dinner that night to Sarah.

"Oh, I met his wife the other day when their furniture was being delivered. She seemed nice enough. They have twin boys and a girl, all three years apart. I can't imagine trying to handle all that."

Five people. Names unknown. They'd apparently been living in the darkened and very quiet house to the west of Dave since the blackout.

Laying low. Getting increasingly desperate.

Running out of food.

Dave heard the fifth gunshot.

He knew there would be no more.

He knelt down and said a prayer for the young family he'd never gotten to know, and hoped they'd have an easier time in heaven.

He stood up and was surprised to find a tear rolling down his cheek.

–42–

He wasn't sure why he was doing it, exactly. It was a very risky move on his part, and he was exposing himself to great violence. It went against all of the plans that he and Sarah had made for three long years.

And it wasn't that he didn't have enough other things to do, either.

The wheat crop was ready to harvest, and the corn wasn't far behind it. He certainly had enough to keep him busy from dawn to dusk for at least the next month.

Something inside of him, though, made him go.

It made him open the gate on the side of his house, in broad daylight, and walk next door to his nameless neighbor's house to the west.

It was the same something that made him knock several times on the front door. Hoping someone would answer. And knowing deep within his soul that it wasn't going to happen.

He'd had a tough time sleeping the night before.

Every time he closed his eyes he could see the children, and imagine what they must have gone through. And he felt like the worst person in the world.

It was easy for him to say that the red headed man and his wife had the same opportunities to prepare that he and Sarah did.

And that was true.

But it was also true that Dave had way more than he needed, since he'd planned for provisions to support four people and three of them weren't there. Yes, the smart thing to do was to conserve as much as he could as long as he could, so that when his family reconciled they'd be in good shape.

But that didn't help him feel better. The bottom line was, he was almost positive that the family next door took their own lives to keep from dying of thirst or starving to death. And he, Dave Speer, could have saved them.

But he didn't.

He felt he had to do something.

It had nothing to do with paying penance. He was quite sure that if God was angry with him for his behavior, he'd burn in hell no matter what he did.

No, it had more to do with a strong desire to do something… anything, to give these people back a semblance of dignity.

When he received no answer at the door, he was convinced his neighbors were dead. He didn't want to raise the ire of his neighbors by breaking into the front of the house.

So he returned to his own yard and secured the gate.

Then he went into his garage and retrieved the saw he'd used to cut secret passages between his yard and the other two yards sharing his fence line.

He might as well make passages in all three sides of the fence.

Within an hour he was at the rear of the neighbor's house, peeking in the windows.

He could plainly see them, lined up on the living room floor. The furniture had been moved aside, so they could lay in repose together.

Now there was no doubt.

He kicked in a window at the back of the house and climbed inside, then went to the living room to examine the carnage.

It seemed rather odd. The mother was on one side and the three children lay in the center. The father lay on the other side. It was as though even in their last moments, the parents were trying to protect their children.

The woman and children each had a gunshot in the center of their foreheads.

The father had placed the gun in his mouth and had blown the top of his head off. The gun was still gripped tightly in his hand.

Dave wondered how the father had gotten his children to lie so straight and still when they knew the end was coming. Then he saw two empty bottles of sleeping pills on the coffee table. He supposed that the children were dead or near death from an overdose when they were shot. The bullets were probably an insurance policy to make sure they didn't wake up and have to fend for themselves after the parents were gone.

Dave had to step back outside and retch.

After his stomach emptied, he returned to the house and went to the master bedroom. He pulled a comforter off the bed and dragged it back to the living room. He used it to cover up the bodies, both to give them a little bit of dignity, and to chase away the flies that had already started to gather on the bodies.

He looked at the children's faces and cried for a moment.

Then he returned to the back yard, picked up his shovel, and started to dig.

-43-

The sun was low in the sky when Dave finally finished digging the mass grave. His back was aching and his arms were on fire. This surpassed even the planting, and was the most physical labor he remembered ever doing in a single day.

He was too exhausted to prepare and move the bodies. That would have to wait until morning.

He climbed out of the hole, which was about six feet long and four feet wide. It was about four feet deep or so. He wasn't sure exactly, but it was over his waist and deep enough to make him struggle to get his weary body out of it.

He stumbled to the fence that separated this yard from his own, and it occurred to him that he walked unlike a zombie. Slowly, deliberately, dragging his feet. He hadn't slept well the night before and hoped he could get some sleep tonight.

Usually, when he and his body were exhausted from a hard day's work, Dave slept very well.

But he knew that every time he'd close his eyes he'd see the faces of those three emaciated children, each with a clean round bullet hole in their little foreheads.

He wasn't sure, but he suspected that the images would haunt him for the rest of his life.

As he crawled through the hole in the fence, one of the rabbits darted through it and into the neighbor's yard.

He was too tired to chase it.

But it did give him an idea.

Dave had no trouble falling asleep that night. His body, in desperate need of recovering after being abused all day, simply pulled rank on his troubled mind.

But that didn't mean he slept well.

He tossed and turned and even woke up once, a little after three a.m.

He'd had a bad dream.

That on the southern outskirts of Kansas City, Sarah's brother Tommy, and his wife Sarah, hadn't planned as well as they though they had.

And they'd run out of provisions.

And that Sarah had made a difficult decision.

In his dream, he saw Sarah, dressed in white, lying on her back. His daughters, Lindsey and Beth, lay on either side of her, her arms wrapped around them. Their heads lay on her breasts in a peaceful pose.

And all three of them had bullet holes in their foreheads.

Dave seldom dreamed. And he almost never had nightmares.

So this one affected him greatly.

Unable to get the ugly vision out of his head, he stumbled out of bed and went into the back yard to urinate.

With every movement, his body screamed in pain, stiff and sore from the previous day's work.

He knew his dream wasn't based in reality. He'd seen Tommy's food stores. He had enough to feed his own family of four for at least three or four years. Yes, the stores would be depleted sooner with three extra mouths to feed, sure.

But Tommy and Susan had an advantage over Dave and Sarah because they lived outside the city. It would be much easier to grow crops, and they had the equipment they needed to grow crops on a large basis.

And they had livestock, too. Six head of cattle and a couple of pigs. And chickens.

Dave didn't want to admit it, although a tiny voice in the back of his mind kept reminding him. But his wife and daughters were probably better off with Tommy and Susan than they would be at home.

He wondered if they worried about his safety and well being as much as he worried about them.

He downed a bottle of water, and the ease at which it went down reminded him he was dehydrated from the day before.

Then he returned to the hole. It was still too dark outside to do anything. So he went back to bed, fully expecting to still be there, wide awake, when the sun came up an hour and a half later.

Instead, he was asleep almost as soon as his head hit the pillow.

He woke up again just before noon. Still sore, his head foggy from lack of water. And he was famished.

The frozen food in the freezer was long gone now, and he was surviving on canned goods. In a way, he preferred them over the frozen food that had to be cooked, or at least heated. Most of the canned goods were just as tasty eaten from the can as they were when heated.

The day before Dave had killed six cans of vegetables to get his daily calorie count. He had to eat them a little at a time throughout the day, and he wondered if the strictly vegetarian diet helped weaken him during the four long hours he was digging the grave.

Today, he needed something more substantial.

He pulled two large cans of Dinty Moore beef stew from a temporary hiding place underneath Beth's old bed. He noted that there were just a few cans left. Soon, he'd have to pull one of the posters from her wall and pull out some more of his long term stock to replenish this day to day pile.

He took the cans of stew to the dining room table and pondered his situation.

It was only a few months before when Sarah had teased him.

"Look at that! You're getting a middle aged spread!"

He'd been standing naked in the bathroom, after stepping out of the shower. Sarah was taking off her makeup and getting ready for bed when she'd noticed his expanding stomach in the mirror.

He looked down, and sure enough, it was getting a bit harder to see his own toes.

She hadn't meant it harshly, of course. She was way too sweet for that. But it did make him think.

Dave had always been proud of his physique. He jogged more than most men, and even went to the gym three days a week to do time on the weight machines or to play basketball. But he had indeed been slowing down in recent months, and had developed a great love for Sarah's good cooking.

He remembered making a mental note to himself to cut back on the second helpings and to increase his jogging distance.

But now, it was a different story.

He'd taken off his shirt while he was upstairs and stepped into the bathroom.

Even in the semi-darkness, it was easy to see his paunch was gone. He hadn't been this slim since he was in the Marine Corps and had no choice.

His stomach had shrunk considerably in the months since the blackout. He knew he wasn't starving. He always counted his calories to make sure he was getting enough.

No, the problem was that his lifestyle had changed. He was no longer leading a mostly sedentary lifestyle, sprawled across the couch all weekend watching three ball games back to back.

He was no longer hitting the all you can eat buffet up the street every weekend, or enjoying Sarah's cooking so much that seconds just wasn't enough.

His stomach had shrunk considerably.

So much so that he was unsure he could eat both cans of beef stew at one sitting.

But he had to try. He needed the fuel to wrap the bodies, and to get them out of the house and into the grave.

He also strongly suspected that he'd have no appetite later, when the deed was done.

Even now, he felt guilty for eating. In his mind he could still see the emaciated corpses of the family who'd gotten so desperate they saw no other way out.

He didn't know if they ran out of food or water first. He hadn't taken the time to look around their house to see what provisions they'd left behind.

He wondered what he'd have done if they'd come knocking on his door, asking for food and water. Would he have ignored them, even though he had plenty? Would he have wanted so much to keep his presence in the neighborhood hidden that he'd let fellow human beings starve to death or die of thirst? Had he sunk that low?

The question was somehow made easier by the fact that they'd never come knocking. He'd never been faced with that horrible decision.

But it still troubled him.

–44–

Hi Baby.

Yesterday was the second worst day since the blackout began. The only day worse than yesterday was the day you and the girls disappeared from my life and got on that plane. The day of the blackout itself. As bad as that day was, this one was almost as bad.

I think this is the fourth of July weekend, although I'm not quite sure because I've sort of lost track of the days. I know I need to do a better job, so I'll know when it's time to harvest the crops and will know when winter is coming. But some days I go to the calendar and honestly can't remember if I already crossed off a day. I don't know if it's my memory that's going, or my mind. Maybe both.

Yesterday I buried Anthony and Sally Nance. Also their three children, Joshua, Jacob and Antoinette. They called her Toni.

I know, you don't have a clue who I'm talking about. Remember the people who moved into 4027, the house next door? He brought over your *Good Housekeeping* magazine when it wound up in his mailbox, remember?

Anyway, I know you never knew their names. I didn't either. It took me a little bit of work to find them. I had to look through the mail they had on their kitchen counter to get Anthony and Sally's names. The kids' names were a little harder. I found a big sign, drawn in crayon, on one of the bedroom doors, that said, "Toni's Room. Yucky Boys Keep Out!!!!!"

Actually, it had three lines of purple exclamation marks. That girl meant business.

I had just about given up on the boys' names, until I found a portrait hanging on the wall with the caption, "Joshua and Jacob, age three."

I know I've lost you, so I'll go back to the beginning.

Four days ago I heard five gunshots, over the course of several minutes. I could tell they were coming from next door.

I've heard enough shots, spaced evenly apart, over the last few months to know what it was. I've come to differentiate a shootout between homeowners and looters, and a family committing suicide. Always before, though, the suicides were down the street, or on the next block, or somewhere off in the distance.

This was different. This was right next door. These were people that you and I actually talked to, but chose not to know.

Something, and I still don't know what, made me go over there. During the daytime. I broke one of our most basic rules of survival, and risked everything, to expose myself in broad daylight.

But like I said, I had to go.

They didn't answer their door. I knew they wouldn't. I wound up breaking into the back of their house.

Looking back, I think it was God telling me to go over there. I think he wanted me to witness what I'd done.

I didn't realize how thin and frail they'd become until it came time to move their bodies. They were withered away to almost nothing.

And I could have saved them.

There was no food in their house. There was a bowl of grass they'd plucked from the yard, on the kitchen counter.

While I was over here, bitching about having to eat green beans and ravioli from cans, they were eating grass from their back yard, in a desperate attempt to stay alive.

They'd turned themselves into little more than cattle, because they so desperately wanted to live. And I had it within my power to save them and didn't.

I have plenty. I could have given them your share, and the girls' share. I could have killed some rabbits for them. I could have done the Christian thing to do, and kept them alive.

And I could have gone a step farther. I could have shared some of our seeds with them. Helped them set up a water collection system, and given them some of my water until the rains came. I didn't do any of that. I was so damn smug in the knowledge that we had planned ahead. We had provisions and plans that would enable us to get by. I had no pity for those who didn't prepare, as we did.

And now I know I'll burn in hell for letting them die. God wanted to show me what I'd done. And here's the thing. I'm okay with it. If anyone deserves an eternity in hell, it's me.

I felt a need to make amends. Or maybe it was another God thing. Maybe He put it in my head that the least I could do was give these people a decent burial.

That's why I needed their names. I wanted to say a prayer for each of them after it was done. And I felt like such a scumbag that I let them die, and didn't even know their names.

I wrapped each of them in a white sheet. For some odd reason, I thought it would hasten their journey to heaven or something, I don't know… or maybe because it made them look more peaceful.

I had to drag Anthony. Although he was only half the size he was when he came knocking on the door that day, he was still too heavy to carry.

I put him in the grave first, then crawled in with him to push his body to one side.

And I apologized to him.

I was able to carry Sally. She was a grown woman, yet she weighed no more than Beth. I placed her on the ground next to the grave and then climbed inside to lower her body down. I know you met her once. I never did, and I found myself wondering what kind of woman she was. I wondered if she was the kind of woman who would forgive me for letting her die.

I placed the children on top of their parents, the boys on the outside and Toni in the middle. Big brothers should always protect their sisters, even in death.

It sounds silly, I know. I know they couldn't feel it. But I just couldn't bring myself to shovel dirt on any of their faces. I filled in the graves by shoveling dirt at their feet. Gravity slowly caused the dirt to roll down off the pile and cover them all up, but I just couldn't shovel dirt into the faces of people who once breathed and laughed and cried.

And who I helped kill.

I said a prayer over the grave when I finished, and asked God to take these good people to heaven with him. I didn't ask for forgiveness, though. I don't feel I deserve it.

It was one of the hardest things I've ever had to do. But here's the thing…

If they had come to my door asking for food and water I likely would have turned them away. I know that. In all the time we were prepping, we went by the prepper's creed, which is, in effect, you can never stock too much or let people know you have extra. You don't know how long it will last or when something will no longer be available. I likely would have sent them away, thinking that I had to conserve our extra food for the day when you and the girls came home.

And as harsh and heartless as it sounds, I know this:

If someone else comes knocking on our door tomorrow I will struggle mightily. Do I help them out and risk them coming back, maybe by force, when they need some more? Do I give them food and water, and risk them telling others I have it?

Or do I refuse to answer the door? Do I let them go away, knowing that they, and possibly their children, might starve to death because I was selfish and greedy?

I know, it's not likely to happen. There's a big sign on the front door that says the house is empty. And anyone looking in the picture window out front will see empty rooms.

But still, I feel like a monster. I feel like I gave up my right to consider myself human when those five people died and I could easily have helped them.

I took ten of the rabbits and put them in a big box. Then I took them out in the front yard last night in the darkness and set them free. There's plenty of grass on the lawns for them to eat, and the morning dew will give them water to drink.

I'm hoping that some of them will make their way down to the storm ditch at the end of the street. There's high grass there and the water pools for weeks after a heavy rain. I have no doubt that most, if not all, will survive.

I also found the literature that the pet store gave us when we bought the rabbits. It's odd that I never read it before.

It turns out that they will start breeding when they're six months old. Each female can have several litters a year, from seven to fifteen babies each time.

That's a boatload of rabbits.

My hope is that after a few months, there will be a few hundred rabbits out there for the survivors to trap or hunt. And that maybe with no stray dogs to threaten them, they'll populate faster than people can kill them. Maybe in five years they'll be the primary source of protein for this whole part of the city.

I did something else too.

I found the literature for the corn we bought. I had a lot left over when I planted the crop, and it turns out that this variety grows from seed to harvest in only seventy two days. I should have known it wasn't long because ours is almost ready to cut.

Anyway, there's still enough time left to plant and harvest a second crop before the winter comes.

I took the seeds that were left when I finished planting, and put aside enough for our own second crop. Then I divided the rest into four equal piles.

I put each pile in a zip lock bag and made four identical signs. Each sign said "Corn seed. Do not eat this. If you eat it, it's only one meal. If you plant it, it will feed you for months."

I also made four identical sets of instructions. I wrote how to prepare the ground, how to catch water in rain buckets, how to plant the seeds, how to water each plant individually and how often.

In other words, I told them everything I've learned from being a farmer so far.

I also told them to plant the seeds immediately so they could harvest their crop before winter. And to save enough seeds from their crop for another planting in the spring.

And I asked them to put aside some of their seeds to share with a stranger, and to ask that stranger to keep it going.

I went out last night, since as I said I couldn't sleep anyway. About a block away I turned over a trash can in the middle of the street. I put a sign and a set of instructions underneath one of the bags.

Then I went another block and did the same thing.

I put the four bags of seeds on four different blocks.

I hope whoever finds them can resist the urge to eat the seeds on the spot.

I didn't have any wheat seeds left over. But the wheat is ready to harvest now, and it's still time to do a second crop. I plan to take some of the seeds from the wheat crop and do the same thing.

Call it my penance for letting those poor people die.

-45-

Dave finally got some sleep the next day. He could have slept through the entire day, but he forced himself out of bed in the early afternoon. He knew if he slept all day he wouldn't be able to sleep that night. And he wanted to get his sleep schedule back on track.

He started his corn harvest that afternoon. He looked through the piles and piles of miscellaneous literature that he and Sarah had printed off the internet in the previous year and a half. There were literally thousands and thousands of pages, and little organization. They basically printed out anything and everything they could find that they thought might be useful, tossed it into several boxes, and left it there to sort later.

During the two nights he couldn't sleep, Dave had sat in his safe room and gone through the boxes by candlelight, sorting and stapling and labeling.

It was in the last box that he found information on how to harvest corn and store it for long term use.

It was grueling work. Cutting the ears of corn from the stalks was the easy part. Removing the corn from the ears would be considerably harder. And it could wait for a few days.

He had to get the second crop in the ground so it could start growing.

After he removed all the cobs from the stalks, he pulled each one up from its roots. The ground was still relatively soft, even after the growing season, and he found that if he worked each stalk back and forth a few times, it came out with just a hard tug.

He took the stalks over to his fence and tossed them over into his own back yard.

By the time he finished, he had a pile of dead corn plants fifteen feet square and eight feet high.

And he made a lot of new friends among his rabbit population. They seemed to love the stuff.

"Don't pig out too much," he said to them as he watched them gorge themselves. "You want to make that stuff last as long as possible, and you're going to have a lot of new mouths to share it with."

He put thirty ears in the garage to dry completely on the cob. That would be his seed supply in the spring.

The rest of the cobs sat in laundry baskets and cardboard boxes in his dining room. He'd process them as soon as his second crops were in the ground.

–46–

Dave very vaguely remembered walking into the office one day and asking what Sarah was researching. It was the day she'd ordered bulk seed from a supplier on Amazon.

"I'm researching the different varieties of corn and wheat," she'd said while looking over her shoulder.

"I didn't know there was a difference. If you can find it, get the kind of corn that's already in cans. I know they grow it that way because it's on the shelves at the grocery store."

"Okay, smartass. If I come across a variety that grows corn in cans, I'll be sure to order that one."

"So, what do you mean, they have different varieties?"

"Well, some corns are sweeter than others. Some have bigger kernels than others. Some grow better in hot and dry climates like we have, and some grow faster than others. Wheat seed is the same way. There are lots of versions of it too."

"So, which kind are you looking for?"

"I'm looking for ones that taste good and that grow well in our climate and grow fast."

"Why fast?"

"Well, duh… so we can plant two crops every year if we need to."

Dave had left the room at that point and gone on to other things.

But he had enough faith in Sarah. She was always meticulous when she did her research, and if there was one thing she was good at it was shopping.

So even though he didn't know much about the corn and wheat seeds she bought, he knew that he had time to grow a second crop of each of them before winter came in a few months and a freeze killed his plants.

But he didn't want to waste any time. He wanted to get the seeds in the ground quickly.

He'd forgotten how hard it was to crawl around on his hands and knees for hours on end. He wished there was a machine that would do this work for him, but there wasn't. He had to do it the way farmers had done it for centuries, before the industrial age came along.

And, he was finding, it was a fairly efficient way of farming.

He did make one modification in the way he planted the second corn crop. He adopted the same method he'd used when he planted his wheat crop, of planting two rows of corn on each side of his work row. He staggered the two corn rows, so that he could reach each plant to water it. But it would almost double his yield for the second crop.

And he made a promise to himself that he would take a portion of the seed and spread it around the neighborhood to help others for the spring planting.

The deaths of the Nance family had changed Dave to a degree. He'd always put his own life and the lives of his family above all others. It had to be that way. He'd do anything to ensure the survival of his wife and daughters. And part of that was making sure he was alive himself to provide for them and to protect them.

But he'd also developed a sense of community. Too many lives had been lost already. He heard gunshots by the dozens, each and every night. And, like the Nances, sometimes during the day too. The smell of death was as strong as ever. And lately, he could smell smoke, off in the distance. It was a putrid smell as well. It wasn't wood burning, like he'd have expected of a house fire. No, this was an ugly smell. Almost as bad as the smell of the decomposing bodies.

And this smell, and the smoke that sometimes blew in on the winds with it, was constant.

It almost reminded Dave of the smell of a badly burned steak, left forgotten on the grill.

After the burning had gone on for a couple of weeks on end, Dave finally figured out what it was.

It was the city of San Antonio, gathering and burning the bodies.

He didn't know when the killing would stop. But he suspected there would be few who survived to the end.

At some point, he knew, the gunshots would have to stop, though. And eventually, the few survivors would start coming out to survey the damage. He hoped there would be no territorial wars or animosity among the survivors. He hoped they would band together for mutual protection and to help each other instead.

He hoped.

On the fourth day of planting the corn, Dave was within sight of finishing up when the clouds came back. He picked up the pace a little, wanting to complete his last row before the rain started to fall.

Rainy days were still exciting to him. He'd had several of them now, and each one represented a lot of work. But he had his collection system down to a science now. He still lost water sometimes, when the rains were so heavy that all of his barrels and bottles were filled and there was nothing left to put it in. But he was confident that he'd have enough water to get him through the rest of the summer months now that the rains were fewer and farther between.

And, he'd noticed when he snuck out of the house a few nights before, the neighbors were learning from him.

He'd gone out to see whether the four bags of seed he left were gone. It had occurred to him that if any were untouched it would mean that all of the people on that street were probably dead. If that were the case, he'd have moved them to another location so they wouldn't have gone to waste.

But he was happy to see that all the seeds were gone. And, apparently the people who took the seeds were also taking his advice on how to collect and preserve rain water.

He noticed that every single one of the large trash cans that had been out on the streets was now gone. There were piles of garbage everywhere, sure. But at least people were using his technique and his seeds to survive. And that in itself gave him a sense of accomplishment.

His luck, and the rains, held.

The first drops hit his face just after he'd planted the very last seed of corn.

For just a few moments, he held his face to the sky and enjoyed the sensation.

Then he was off to the races. First to the trash cans he'd turned into rain barrels at the back of the Hansen house. When he'd gathered up the trash cans from the streets, he'd left the lids behind. Many of them were missing anyway, and gathering them would have meant more exposure time, Instead, he'd put strips of plastic tarp over the cans and held them into place with bungee cords, to keep the water from evaporating between rainfalls.

At the Hansen house, he pulled the tarp off and cast it aside. The new rain came washing down the roof and into the barrels, replacing the water he'd been using for irrigation.

Then he scampered over to the Castro house and did the same thing.

Those barrels were mostly full. He'd pumped water from three of them to replenish the ones in the Hansen yard. Hopefully the rain would refill those three barrels and would agitate the water in the other full barrels enough to kill any mosquito larvae growing in them.

Finally, Dave went back to his own yard and removed the lids from his own trash cans. As they started to fill, he ran inside the house to get several bags of two liter soda bottles that he'd emptied since the previous rain.

He dipped each bottle below the water level to refill it, then replaced the cap and set it aside.

He hoped there were many others around the neighborhood doing the same thing.

–47–

The best thing about the rain was that it gave Dave the ability to survive for a few more months.

The second best thing was that it gave him the excuse to take a much needed break.

The rain came down in torrents for three straight hours. Every one of the rain barrels, at all three houses, was now full and overflowing. Every container Dave had was full as well, including both of the bathtubs and all the sinks in his house.

As the rain slowed, he stood, dripping wet, and surveyed the corn plot he'd just planted. The new seeds had gotten the gift of life from the heavy rain. They'd start to soften, and in a few days they'd start to sprout.

And the life cycle would begin anew.

As for the wheat crop that needed to be harvested, and was next on his list of things to do, that would have to wait for a couple of days.

The work rows between the rows of wheat were just too muddy to be slogging around in. And although Dave didn't know too much about farming, even he knew that the wheat couldn't be harvested while it was damp. It had to be completely dry, to prevent the crop from being mildewed and ruined.

So he had an excuse. He could rest at least a day, maybe two, without feeling guilty. He could sleep late, and let his aching bones and exhausted muscles recover.

And, he decided, he'd even treat himself.

While he was on his break and resting with not much to do, he'd double the amount of generator time. After all, gasoline was plentiful. He'd refilled his gas cans the last time he was out at night, and there were dozens more cars here and there with gas in their tanks.

So for the next day or two he'd be able to watch two John Wayne movies per day instead of one. Or watch twice as many family videos. And he'd feel the cooling wind from the floor fan chilling his sweaty face as he sat on his bed and watched the movies.

In a perfect world, he'd be enjoying his brief respite with Sarah and his girls.

But then again, in a perfect world the EMP never would have struck and the blackout never would have happened.

The world was far from perfect. In fact, the world at present was still a dangerous and ugly place.

But at least for the next day or two, it would be tolerable.

-48-

Hi honey.

I just got back. It's less than an hour before sunrise, and I plan to sleep most of the day. So I thought I'd spend a few minutes with you first, or at least as long as my flashlight holds out, before I hit the rack.

I went out to the streets again tonight. I know, I know, that was something we were never supposed to do.

But something keeps making me go out there. I don't know if it's my own guilt, or some higher power making me go out to atone for letting the Nances die. Whatever it is, I can't help it. I'm sorry, but I can't.

This time I delivered bunnies.

Let me explain.

A few days ago I was in the back yard on my way back from the Hansen house. I'd just finished picking some fresh tomatoes and cucumbers from the garden and was going to eat them for dinner along with my rabbit soup.

The oddest thing happened, though. One of the rabbits… not one of the original ones we started out with, but one of the first litter, came over to me and just stood there in front of me, looking at me. I walked toward her, and she held her ground, like she was challenging me.

I went to go around her and she moved too. Then I moved back the other way, and so did she.

I thought I was losing my mind, but it was almost like she didn't want me to pass. Or she was trying to tell me something.

I knelt down to see if she'd let me pet her, and surprisingly she did. I thought that was odd because usually the rabbits all scatter when I'm around.

Anyway, she let me pet her, and that's when I noticed she was very pregnant.

I'd forgotten how quickly the rabbits reproduce. And I started looking at some of the other rabbits as well. It's hard to tell which ones are females from a distance, because you can't see… well, you know. But several of them appeared to be extra plump.

It occurred to me that I need to take steps to keep the rabbit population under control, or I'm going to be overrun. I mean, we knew that the rabbits we had would produce an offspring of as many as six hundred rabbits the first year. We didn't see that as a problem. We figured that between the four of us, we could eat most of them. And that we could turn the rest into jerky to add to our dry stock or to barter later on.

But I can't eat six hundred rabbits in a year. And drying out rabbit meat over an open fire is time consuming.

When I was in Jack Castro's garage looking for supplies, I remembered seeing three small dog cages. The kind you put your dogs in when you take them to the vet.

As far as I knew, they never had any dogs. I mean, I never heard any barking or anything. And these cages had plenty of dust on them, like they hadn't been used in awhile.

Anyway, long story short, I went back and got those three cages. And in each cage I put two pregnant bunnies and one male.

The girls would have laughed their asses off, watching me chase those bunnies around the yard. I think they've learned that whenever they see me pick up one of them, they never see that particular bunny again. So they run from me now.

Needless to say, it took awhile to catch them. Especially the males. They had a lot more energy than the pregnant females.

Anyway, I wrote out three signs and taped them to the top of each cage.

The signs said to resist the urge to eat the rabbits. Rather, to let them breed. I said they would eat grass or most other green things, and didn't need a lot of water. I said if they let the babies happen, they'd be mature enough to eat in just a few months. I also said that the mama would be pregnant again within a few weeks and would have her next litter six weeks after that.

Lastly, I asked them to pay it forward. I asked them to decide when they had enough of a rabbit population to support their needs, and then to do the same thing I did. That they put two pregnant females and a male back into the cage and leave it out to share with another family.

Other than that, there's not a lot of things going on here.

Had to take a break and wait for daylight. My flashlight batteries went dead. Sorry about that.

I'm finding that it takes forever for the rechargeable batteries to recharge, just charging for an hour and a half a day. I think when the weather starts to cool in a few weeks, I'll start using candles. That'll help. Right now, though, it's too damn hot in here as it is.

I noticed yesterday that the second corn crop is starting to sprout its ears. I'll be able to harvest it in a few more weeks. The second wheat crop is waist high now, and coming along nicely. I anticipate that both will be ready to harvest before the first freeze.

So all in all, I guess things are going fairly smoothly here. I love you, hon. Please give the girls each a kiss from me and tell them I love them too. I miss you so bad it hurts. But I'll survive. I have to.

–49–

Dave checked the garden. The vegetables were growing faster than he could eat them. He could exceed his daily calorie count, of course. But he didn't want to do that for a couple of reasons. First of all, he was strong and had sufficient energy on most days to do the chores that needed to be done. He didn't need any extra energy. So any additional calories he took in would merely be wasted.

Secondly, he'd never given up on his dream to somehow find his family and bring them back with him. And if he was successful in doing that, they'd still need whatever food he could stockpile. He knew it might take several weeks for him to make it to Kansas City. And several more weeks to get back.

He also knew he couldn't make the trip in the wintertime. The ice and snow would just make it too treacherous. And it would be too easy for someone to follow him on snow covered ground.

No, the smart time for him to set out would be the springtime. Which meant he'd be on the move instead of planting and caring for his crops.

Which meant that when he returned with Sarah and the girls, they'd have less food to eat, without the two additional crops of corn and two crops of wheat.

And that, no matter which way he figured it, meant he still had to conserve food wherever he could. Because when he returned with his family the following summer, they had to have enough food to live on at least until the following spring when they could plant again.

So eating extra calories just for the sake of preventing the vegetables from going to waste was just not an option.

Instead, he revisited his plan to store drinking water in the bottom of his chest freezer, hidden beneath a bunch of spoiled and rancid food.

He went to the garage and opened the freezer. He slammed it shut again a lot more quickly.

The food was already spoiled when he put it in there. Unable to dry out, it then mildewed and the smell grew exponentially worse.

It was so bad he wanted to vomit.

In his mind he debated whether it was even worse than the decaying bodies that permeated the air around him.

He decided that the mass of stinking decay had to go. And the only place he could put it to keep from stinking was in the ground.

So he went to the center of his back yard and dug a hole, two feet deep and two feet square.

A couple of the rabbits jumped into it as soon as he finished, happy that this human finally decided to stop eating them and decided to help them to dig their tunnels instead.

Dave didn't bother removing them. He knew it would be a lost cause. They'd merely jump back in as soon as he was out of view.

Instead, he walked up the stairs to the medicine chest in the bathroom and took out the Vick's Vapor Rub.

Sarah used to rub it on the girls' chests when they were congested, to help them sleep better at night.

But Dave had a different plan for it.

He stuck his finger into the heavy paste and took a large dollop of it out of the jar, then rubbed it between his upper lip and nose.

It burned his nose. But the smell was pleasant, and immediately blocked out all other smells.

Next, he put on some rubber gloves from the kitchen and went into the garage, where he scooped the disgusting muck from the freezer into a large garbage bag.

He carried the bag at arm's length to the back yard, where he placed it next to the hole.

He'd expected to have to reach into the hole to remove several rabbits before he could place the bag inside the hole.

But it turned out that the rabbits didn't like the awful smell either. As soon as he brought the bag out the door, they scattered to the far corners of the yard in an attempt to get away from whatever was in the bag.

Dave couldn't blame them a bit.

But that wasn't all. The smell was so bad inside the freezer that even the bottles of water reeked of it. Even though there was a sheet of heavy plastic that separated them from the spoiled food and they never actually came in contact with it.

Dave took the bottles over to the garden. The crops were only a couple of weeks from harvesting now, but the water in these bottles would never be consumed. It would be used to irrigate the crops for their last few days.

The inside of the freezer also reeked, until Dave washed it down with straight Clorox bleach. Then he left the freezer door open for a couple of days before rinsing it.

His plan was to harvest the rest of the vegetables and berries from the vegetable garden, and to freeze as many as he could. He was confident that running the freezer an hour and a half per day would be enough. He'd tested it, in fact. He knew that normally the condenser on a chest freezer would come on periodically throughout the day to drop the temperature down to the desired level. Then it would turn off again for several hours.

Dave found that when the freezer was only powered for ninety minutes a day, it ran pretty much non-stop, but was indeed able to reach the desired setting on the thermostat.

The well-insulated freezer walls and door kept the temperature from rising too much during the other twenty two and a half hours a day.

Dave simply reset the thermostat to twenty degrees. When the condenser was running, it worked hard to lower the temperature to that level. And once it was that cold, the insulation kept it cold. It seldom rose over thirty degrees the rest of the day.

He knew he had too many vegetables to fit in the freezer, though, so he was simultaneously working to dry out many of them.

He used a system Sarah had found in a prepper's book. Dave still remembered the day he walked into the bedroom and found her reading it.

"What are you reading, hon?"

"Oh, it's a book called *Prepping for Armageddon on a Budget*. I think you'll like it. It was written by a former Marine like yourself. And it has all kinds of tips for prepping that don't cost an arm and a leg."

"Too late. I've already spent two arms and one leg. That's why I move so slow."

"Very funny. No, seriously. There's some good stuff in here. Right now I'm learning how to dry out the vegetables from our garden so they'll be shelf stable and will last for years."

The process was simple enough.

He used the same stew pots he boiled his drinking water in. Only this time he filled them with sliced or chunked vegetables.

He took the stew pots and placed them atop a folding table in his back yard, covered with screens to keep the flies out.

Then he let the sun do its thing, heating the aluminum pots and drying out the vegetables inside.

He stirred each pot several times a day to allow the vegetables on the bottom an equal chance to dry, and brought them inside at night so they wouldn't absorb water from the morning dew.

By the third day in the sun, the vegetables were dehydrated, completely free of moisture, and were shelf stable. They would last for years, stored in plastic zip lock bags.

But whenever Dave needed them for a pot of soup or rabbit stew, just a few minutes of boiling reconstituted them and made them edible again.

–50–

It was late September when Dave noticed it was starting to get cooler in the evenings.

He was glad. He'd had enough of the hot weather. In the dog days of summer it was unbearably hot in his safe room. There were times he was tempted to place a cot in the middle of the back yard and sleep there instead.

But then he remembered the stray bullet hole he found in his fence, and a second one he found in the side of his house later. And he decided the safest place to sleep was in the safe room, despite the overbearing heat.

The day was quickly coming when he'd no longer have plants to irrigate every other day. Yet most of his rain barrels were still full or partially so. And it occurred to him that since he had plenty of water to get him to the spring rains, he could begin using some of it for other purposes.

He employed an old trick he'd learned as a boy, when he'd camp with the boy scouts. He used it later on, too, when he was a United States Marine stationed in Iraq. He started taking off his t-shirt and saturating it with water, then putting it back on when he went to bed. The wet t-shirt kept him cool enough to enable him to fall asleep.

Sometimes, when the heat was particularly oppressive, he'd wake up halfway through the night when his t-shirt was dry. Then it was just a matter of resoaking it. The tactic worked quite well to get him through some otherwise sleepless nights.

Still, he was glad when he noticed the nights were getting cooler. He was by nature a winter person, in that he preferred cold weather over the heat.

But the cooler nights also reminded him that he had three major projects that had to be finished before the heat went away.

He was irrigating the crops and garden every other day. Because each plant had to be watered individually, it was an all-day process. But it left every other day free to do other things.

So on his off-days, the days he didn't irrigate, he spent his time preparing his winter supply of drinking water.

Dave had two good reasons for revisiting his water situation.

First of all, the hundreds of bottles of water he had squirreled all over the property were too full for winter. In an effort to stockpile as much water as possible during the rainstorms, he'd filled each bottle all the way to the top.

And that was fine for the warm weather months.

But Dave was well aware that the two liter soda bottles he stored his bulk water in had no room to expand, like the smaller water bottles did.

That meant at the first freeze, every one of the soda bottles would burst. The water would go to waste, and the bottles would be in shreds and worthless the following spring, when he'd need them again.

The solution was daunting, but necessary. He had no choice but to empty one third of each bottle, to allow the other two thirds room to expand when it froze into ice.

The other reason to revisit his water situation was because it took five times as much fuel to boil a pot of water for ten minutes when it was thirty degrees outside than when it was eighty degrees. Another thing he'd learned in the boy scouts. In the winter, it took longer to cook anything, because the heat from the fire was competing with the cold air temperature around it. In warm weather months that wasn't a problem.

Dave knew that boiling his rainwater in the winter time to make it safe to drink was a bad idea. Therefore, he decided to boil enough of it, when the weather was still hot, to last him through the winter and into springtime.

So on the days when Dave watered the crops, he used the soda bottles instead of the water from the rain barrels. He needed two hundred empty bottles, so he could pour one third of the water from the other bottles into them. He needed another two hundred bottles to hold purified water that was safe to drink over the winter.

It was a lot of work, retrieving the bottles from their hiding places and lugging them outside to the garden. But it had to be done. Unfortunately, Dave saw this as an annual event in the future, much like the plantings and harvests. It would be labor intensive each time, and not something he'd look forward to. But he saw it as an essential part of survival.

He took the first two hundred empty bottles, removed the caps, and let them dry completely in the afternoon sun over the course of two days. He was pretty sure that would kill all of the bacteria inside, but as an added measure he planned to add two drops of chlorine bleach to each bottle as he filled it.

He took a sharpie and wrote a large "D" on all two hundred bottles. The "D" stood for drinking water. It would be his method for deciding which bottles were safe to drink over the course of the winter.

On the days when he wasn't irrigating the crops, his little camp stove was going full bore on his back deck, heating water in the stew pots to the boiling point. And then continuing to boil for an additional ten minutes.

After each pot cooled, he poured it into the marked bottles, added two drops of bleach to each, and returned them to their hiding places.

While he was waiting for the water to boil and cool, he retrieved the rest of the full bottles from here and there and poured one third of each into the second two hundred bottles he'd emptied.

When he was finished, he'd go into the winter season with the same number of bottles he had before. Only this time each would be only two thirds full, and many would be safe to drink from.

But the water was only one of his winter prep projects.

Another would prove to be equally time consuming. And perhaps a little bit more dangerous.

He built his safe room around the fireplace in his den, specifically so he could use it for warmth during the winter months.

The problem was, they only had half a cord of firewood, stacked up against the side of the house, when the EMP hit.

And half a cord wouldn't be enough.

So Dave would have to gather more wood from the only place it was available.

The empty houses around him.

-51-

Dave felt a bit guilty when he walked into the Hansen house with a saw, hammer and crow bar, with the intention of dismantling it.

After all, it was one thing to utilize the back yard to grow his crops, and the rain water that came off the roof to water those crops. It was okay, in his mind, to use this place as a bug out location in the event he was ever overrun.

None of those things caused any damage to the property.

But this, this was different. He was actually here to destroy something that belonged to someone else. Just to make himself a bit more comfortable when the cold weather hit.

Oh, his guilt wouldn't stop him. He knew the world had changed. He knew the bank which owned this property no longer really existed. He knew that no one would challenge him, or ask him to stop.

So even though this went against everything he believed in, it wouldn't deter him.

It would just make him feel bad while he was doing it.

He'd thought out the method of the project the night before while he was lying in bed. He knew it was a bad idea to remove the studs from the downstairs walls first. If he done so, the weight of the upper floor and roof would eventually have been too great for the weakened lower floor to handle. And it would have come crashing down on Dave's head.

No, it made much more sense to go into the attic first. And to carefully remove selected support beams. One at a time, evenly distributed across the length and breadth of the attic.

He did some rough calculations, and figured he could get several hundred board feet of two by fours and two by sixes, before the roof started to sag.

Coupled with the firewood he already had, that might be enough to get him through a mild winter.

But he couldn't rely on the winter being mild. The climate had been changing, even before the EMP, and winters had been a lot more harsh lately.

And it seemed that the last couple of winters lasted longer than normal, too.

No, he'd hope for a mild winter and prepare for a bad one. It was the prudent thing to do.

He'd pull wood out of the attic until the roof started to sag, and then he'd get the hell out of there.

On the second floor, he'd remove every third stud from each of the interior walls. He figured that doing so would weaken the structure, but not so much it would collapse. And the studs from the second floor would provide him the additional wood he'd need to get through the winter.

The following year, gathering the wood from the structure would be a lot harder. Then, it would be weakened and a lot more prone to collapse.

But that was a problem for the following year. Here, now, he'd proceed cautiously, and hopefully wouldn't endanger his life.

–52–

Hi Sugar.

I almost didn't pick up my pen tonight. I was having what you used to call a pity party, and was feeling sorry for myself. I was disgusted because I'm so lonely and miserable and sometimes I really struggle with all that has to be done.

In the midst of that, I almost threw this journal away. I got the sense it was a waste of time. It's something you'll probably never see, or want to see.

I fully expect to come and get you next year. And on our trip back here we'll have plenty of time to talk about everything I've done and experienced since you left. Just like you'll have time to tell me everything you and the girls have done.

By the time you get back here, there won't be any reason for you to read these words.

So in a short fit of rage, I actually threw this book across the room and called myself stupid for writing it. In fact, I almost tore it into little pieces.

Almost.

Then I slowly got over feeling sorry for myself and realized a couple of things. First of all, you guys are going through hardships as well. I know that since Tommy and Susan live outside the city, you don't have to deal with some of the things I do, like the looters and the stench of bodies.

But I also know that living with others, even when they're family, can be stressful in its own right. And I know that it takes a lot of hard work to provide and care for so many people, and I know you're pulling your share of the load. In fact, knowing you like I do, I'm sure you're pulling way more than your share.

And I know that the winters in Kansas City are much worse than they are here. I remember that Christmas we spent up there with Tommy and Susan in their old house, before they moved outside the city. Remember, we were scheduled to fly back and they had a vicious snow storm? We were stranded for four extra days and the city came to a standstill. I hope to God that you don't have to endure a winter like that one.

So as bad as it is down here, I know now that I'm not the only one who's suffering.

No more pity parties for me, I promise.

The other thing that kept me from tearing up this journal was the realization that I'm writing it for myself as much as for you. Even if you never see it, it's our time together. That may sound odd, but when I write in this thing it feels like I'm talking to you. And this will sound really bizarre, but I feel something else too. When I write in this journal, it's almost like you're here with me.

In other words, I've decided that this book is therapeutic for me. It actually helps me get through the hard times emotionally.

I'm so glad I didn't destroy it.

Okay, that was a five cent comment that I stretched into a fifty dollar novel. That wasn't even the reason I picked up my pen tonight.

The reason I decided to write you tonight was because I wanted to tell you what I did today. You'll never believe it.

Remember that charcoal powered camping oven you bought on the internet? The one I made fun of? I remember telling you that you were nuts, and that you couldn't bake bread with charcoal.

And you proved me wrong by baking two loaves of the most delicious bread I've ever tasted.

Well, I pulled that oven out of the garage today. I found the recipe you used for sweet bread, and even though I'm not kitchen literate at all, I was able to find the flour and all the other ingredients and put them all together.

And I managed to put the layer of charcoal in the pan beneath the oven and get it lighted without burning down the deck.

Regulating the temperature was the hardest thing. You probably experienced the same thing. I started out checking the internal thermometer every five minutes or so, but it kept going above or below 350 degrees, and I kept having to crank the charcoal pan either higher or lower each time.

I finally got smart and just sat there, raising and lowering the pan every time the temperature changed.

It was kind of a pain in the ass, to be honest. But it was worth it. Before long the smell of fresh baked bread began drifting out of the vents and actually covered up the dead body smell for a time.

I ate a whole loaf. Seriously. I wrapped the first loaf in wax paper and put it in the freezer with the vegetables. But I couldn't resist with the second loaf. I didn't even slice it. I just tore off a chunk and it melted in my mouth. And it tasted exactly like yours did.

Anyway, one thing led to another, and before you know it the whole loaf was gone. And no, I don't feel guilty about that. Later on I regretted it, because I used up my whole calorie allotment on one loaf of bread. But it was so worth it.

The only difference between mine and yours was that mine didn't rise as high as yours. I looked at the jar of yeast I used, and it's still good for two more years. So I guess I just didn't let it sit on the counter long enough.

I'll get better as I go. For now, though, I know I am capable of baking bread, and may even tackle one of your other recipes soon. The zucchini nut bread sounds good. And we just happen to have zucchini in the garden and pecans on the Hansen's tree.

Sorry, I had to gush a bit. I never in a million years thought I'd be baking bread, of all things.

It's amazing what you can accomplish when you have to.

I love you.

–53–

It was early October now, and Dave had just finished bringing in the second corn crop. Like before, the ears were piled into laundry baskets and cardboard boxes and stacked into a big pile in his dining room.

He'd learned a few things when he processed the first batch of corn. First, he learned that using a knife to cut the kernels off the cobs was a time consuming and dangerous proposition. He cut the same thumb twice during the process.

He'd learned that it was much easier to unshuck the cobs, then to let them dry out, before processing them. Once they were completely dry, he could twist them to make the kernels fall out of the cobs instead of cutting them off.

Lastly, he learned that twisting four hundred cobs of corn was hard work, especially on his forearms. He fully expected to resemble Popeye the Sailor after a couple more harvests.

He was in no hurry to process the second batch of corn. He had a long winter ahead of him, with no crops to care for. He had plenty of time to work the corn pile, and in fact could even do it a little at a time.

So he shifted his focus to the wheat.

He processed the wheat in a completely different manner, while still in the field.

By going down his work rows one at a time, and by cutting off the grains with a small linoleum knife, he could get a good sized handful of wheat kernels, still in the husks.

Then he repeatedly beat the husks against the inside of a large bucket he dragged along behind him. Beating the husks caused the kernels to fall free and settle in the bottom of the bucket. Once the husks were empty, he tossed them aside and gathered another handful.

It was a very slow, but very effective process. He and Sarah had already stockpiled a hundred five pound bags of flour for making bread and hard tack after the blackout. It was stored in zip-lock storage bags in the wall of the garage, hidden behind a sheet of sheetrock.

He wasn't sure how much flour this crop would make after he ground it. But he was fairly confident it would stretch the existing stock of flour considerably, even though he'd now developed the capability to bake bread with it.

He figured another week or more to finish bringing in the wheat crop. Then he'd pull the plants up by the roots, along with the corn plants and the plants from the garden that no longer bore vegetables.

He'd toss all the vegetation over the fence into his own back yard, where it would feed his ever expanding population of rabbits over the winter months.

After three days of crawling around on his hands and knees, though, he decided he needed a break.

As he had done before with the corn, he took four zip-lock sandwich bags, and poured about a cup of wheat seeds into each.

Then he made a sign to place underneath the bag of seeds:

PLEASE DON'T EAT THESE SEEDS
If you eat them, they'll only provide one meal.
But if you save them until the springtime and plant them, the wheat they will produce will feed you for months. Here's how:

1. Trap rain in barrels and trash cans during the spring rains. Put them against your house, where they will catch the runoff from your roof.

2. Cover the cans when they're not in use, so the water doesn't evaporate.

3. Prepare the ground by digging it up and then removing all grass and roots.

4. Plant seeds one at a time, one inch deep and eight to ten inches apart.

5. Water each plant, every other day. On days you have a good rain, skip three days.

6. Harvest when the stalks hang low and dry out.

7. If you plant in late March, you can harvest in June and plant a second crop. The two crops together will feed several people for several months.

8. After your second harvest, be sure you save seeds for your next planting in the spring.

9. TAKE SOME MORE OF YOUR SEEDS AND SHARE THEM WITH A NEIGHBOR. TELL THEM TO KEEP IT GOING UNTIL EVERYONE HAS THEIR OWN CROPS.

Dave wasn't a long winded guy by nature. But he wanted to be specific. He didn't want anyone's crops dying in the field because they didn't get all the grass roots out of the ground, or water them often enough.

He didn't realize how detailed his instructions were until he had to write out three more copies of the sign long-hand, and it gave him writer's cramp.

But sore hands were a small price to pay for what he'd come to consider his calling: sharing what he had anonymously with others in the neighborhood, and helping others to survive.

He'd planned on going out that night to deposit the seeds at various locations around the neighborhood. But as he was putting the packages of seeds into a black backpack, he heard a vicious firefight, with AK-47 and AR-15 rifles, only a block or two away. The battle raged for half an hour, and culminated in several blasts from a shotgun.

Dave would never know who was shooting at who, of course. Or why.

But it reminded him that the world outside his home was still a very vicious and violent place.

He also suspected that tensions would be high among the survivors of the shootout, and they'd probably be watching out for more trouble.

He decided to wait a couple more days to complete his seed mission.

–54–

Dave went ahead and finished his wheat harvest. He'd gotten considerably more than the first harvest, and didn't know why. He'd planted the seeds the same way. Watered them on the same schedule.

He wondered if planting the first crop in the early spring, when the ground was still cool from the winter, stunted the growth of the first crop.

Whatever was the cause, he was pleasantly surprised at the yield. And he was happy enough about it to share more of it with neighbors.

When he set out on that Tuesday evening, just before midnight, the black canvas pack on his back contained eight ziplock bags of seeds, and eight identical sets of instructions.

As had been his habit in the past, he first went up the stairs to the front window that overlooked the street. With his night vision goggles in place, he scanned the street for several minutes for the slightest movement or sign of life.

All he saw were the trees blowing, and an occasional odd piece of trash rolling down the street.

He went into his darkened garage and pulled the cord that released the door from the garage door opener.

The overhead door could now be opened manually.

He eased it up about eighteen inches and crawled underneath it.

He was immediately struck by the cool wind. Winter was right around the corner. He wondered if he should have brought a light jacket, and for a brief moment thought about going back.

Then he remembered he didn't even own a black jacket. And the walk would keep him warm.

He pulled the door back down, shouldered his AR-15, and stealthily low crawled away from the house and to the shrubs next door.

From there he once again surveyed the street. And once again he saw no sign of movement.

Then Dave was on his way, moving in short bursts from one set of shrubs or parked car to another.

At first he was disheartened to see that there were no more trash cans as far as he could see, in either direction. Then he realized that was a good thing. It meant that the survivors had taken his advice, or maybe discovered on their own, that they could use the cans to catch rain water.

The only problem was, the lack of cans gave Dave no place to leave the seed packs, as he had done before.

He solved that problem by placing the first package on the hood of a yellow Honda Civic, stalled in the middle of the street, about two blocks from his house.

He tucked the first of the notes underneath the seeds and turned to leave when he heard a man's voice, calling out behind him.

"Hey!"

Dave froze. His back was to the voice, and he was vulnerable. His rifle was over his shoulder and his handgun was still holstered. The man behind him had the drop on him.

If the man meant him harm, Dave was in deep trouble.

But there was something in the tone of the man's voice, in that single word, that struck Dave as nonthreatening. He slowly turned around.

The first human he'd seen up close in eight months was walking toward him, seemingly unarmed, hands outstretched.

What he said next puzzled Dave.

"It's nice to finally get a chance to meet you."

"Excuse me?"

"The whole neighborhood's been talking about you. The mysterious man who comes in the night and leaves seeds, and rabbits, and shares information on how to survive. That's you, right?"

"I guess."

"Are you the same one who released a bunch of rabbits into the wild? I've been seeing them around here quite often lately."

"Yes. I want them to multiply so they eventually provide a source of protein for the survivors."

"Well, I'll be damned. I knew it. I bet old Bill five bucks you were the one. Not that five bucks means anything anymore. But I told him there couldn't be more than one man around these parts who knew how to breed rabbits. It must be you, I said."

The man reached out his hand.

"Frank Woodard. My wife Eva and I live in the blue house right there. Well, it's blue in the daytime. Guess at night it's as black as all the others."

Dave was caught off guard by the man's demeanor. But he shook the hand offered to him.

"I'm Dave. I live… well, back that way a ways."

Frank laughed.

"Let me show you something, Dave. Don't get too jumpy, I'm not reaching for a gun."

He slowly reached into his pocket and pulled out what appeared to be a wallet. Until he opened it up and Dave could see a badge.

"Bexar County Sheriff, twenty one years. I'm sworn to protect and serve. You have nothing to fear from me. But these days it's wise not to give out too much information. So I don't blame you for not wanting to be very specific."

"I'm sorry… Frank. You're the first person I've talked to since the blackout. I don't know what's going on out here, or who I can trust."

"I assume you're a prepper too?"

Dave was caught off guard by the question. He didn't know how to respond.

Frank laughed.

"I'll assume from the night vision goggles and bunny rabbits and seeds that you are. It's okay. I am too. But I have to say I'm impressed about the whole rabbit thing. I wish I'd thought of keeping them myself.

"Since you're out of the loop, Dave, let me fill you in on some things. Like I said, I'm a prepper too. One of the things I saved from the magnetic blast was a ham radio. It was always a hobby of mine. There are twenty of us around the city and county who have working radios, and we've been sharing notes.

"FEMA is on the scene. Don't ask me how, but they've got working helicopters and vehicles. Not many, and I don't know how they got them, but maybe it's one of those things you just shouldn't ask.

"Anyway, they're saying they don't have a lot of resources to pass out, but they're going house to house pulling out dead bodies. They're putting them in the streets in big piles and burning them. They say it's to prevent disease from spreading and killing the survivors. Although I haven't decided yet which is worse. The stench from the bodies or the stench from the fires."

Dave pondered the information carefully. It pretty much confirmed what he'd suspected.

He didn't know why, but he blurted out some information he shouldn't have.

"They probably bypassed the onboard computer and installed a new ignition."

"Beg your pardon?"

Dave regretted opening his mouth, but the cat was out of the bag now. And he felt he could trust this friendly sheriff's deputy, so he went on.

"If they saved the right parts in a Faraday cage, they could replace some of the components on a vehicle and get it running again. All they'd need is a good starter solenoid, a new ignition switch, fuses and battery. They could bypass everything else and run the new ignition directly through the battery to the starter."

"Well, I'll be damned. That's another thing I never thought about."

Dave looked worried, even through the goggles.

"Don't worry, friend. I'll keep that bit of information to myself. I'll assume you just heard that rumor, and have no working car parts yourself."

Dave breathed a sigh of relief.

"Yes. That's right."

Frank smiled a broad smile that Dave sensed was genuine.

"I won't keep you, Dave. You have a reputation to maintain, so I'll let you be on your way. We'll talk another time, I hope. I won't invade your territory. But Eva and I are always here if we can help you in any way."

"What did you mean, I have a reputation to maintain?"

"Oh, I guess you really don't know, do you?"

"Know what?"

"The survivors… there are only a few dozen within a square mile now. They've pretty much relegated you to sainthood. They call you 'God's messenger that comes in the night.' They don't know who you are, but they know of your work. And they appreciate it."

"Oh, it's nothing, really. Just a desire to share what I have."

"Don't sell yourself short, Dave. Whether you know it or not, you've saved a lot of lives. And even more than that, you've restored hope. A lot of families have crops of corn and wheat now to get them through the winter. They have a means to collect water. They're getting protein occasionally by eating one of the rabbits. It's not much to you, but to them it's everything in the world."

Dave didn't know what to say.

Frank held out his hand again and Dave took it.

"As I said, I won't keep you. But I will offer my help. Anything you need that I can do to help your cause, you say the word. You can find me here, day and night."

"Okay, Frank. I'll remember that, and thank you."

"No problem. Keep doing what you're doing, my friend, and God bless you."

Dave finished his rounds, leaving the rest of the seed bags on various abandoned cars around the neighborhood. He was surprised to find out there were so few survivors left.

And he hoped the ones who were left could make it through the harsh winter to come.

There had been enough dying already.

Thank you for reading

ALONE, Book 1.

It was a fun book to write. I hope you enjoyed it.

The next book in this series will be titled

ALONE, Book 2

AN UNKIND WINTER

In *An Unkind Winter*, Mother Nature plays a cruel trick by delivering one of the harshest winters on record. Dave joins forces with Frank and Eva to help the weaker of the neighbors survive from day to day.

Not everybody makes it.

But Dave does, and he misses Sarah and the girls more and more with each passing day.

He finally can't stand the separation any more and starts planning his incredible journey, a thousand miles to the north, to retrieve his family and bring them back home.

ALONE, Book 2

AN UNKIND WINTER

Will be available on Amazon.com and through Barnes and Noble Booksellers in October, 2014.

Please enjoy this preview of

BREAKOUT :

BREAKOUT

is Book 3 in the "Final Dawn" series, and is available now at Barnes and Noble.com and Amazon.com

Hannah hadn't slept in a real bed for a very long time. For six and a half years she and Mark had slept on a four inch mattress in the back of a recreational vehicle, deeply hidden within an abandoned salt mine.

Oh, the mattress wasn't that bad. Not really. And considering that most of the world was dying outside the mine while she was able to sleep safely at night, she really had nothing to complain about.

But now that the group had finally broken out of the mine and ventured out into a brave new world, Hannah was looking forward to a real bed, soft and warm and big enough to stretch out in.

And now, on their very first night outside the mine and in a nearby walled compound, she was sleeping like a baby.

Was.

But not any more.

Little Markie, almost six and a total mini-me of his father, crawled into bed beside her and poked his finger into her cheek. Three times.

"Mommy, are you awake?"

Hannah was now somewhere between slumber and consciousness, in that foggy zone where one isn't sure whether or not they're dreaming.

But she sure hoped she was.

Then she felt it again. The tapping of the finger. And the accompanying words: "Mommy, are you awake?"

"No, honey. Mommy is sleeping."

Please be a dream. Please be a dream.

"Mommy, I'm afraid."

Nothing gets a mother's attention faster than a child who's afraid. Hannah's eyes were instantly open, her mind immediately searching for whatever had frightened her dear child.

She looked at Markie, lying in the bed beside her.

"Afraid of what, little sailor?"

"I don't like this place. I want to go home."

Her heart sank.

She lifted up the covers so little Markie could crawl inside with her and Mark. Then she patted her pillow. "Lay your little head right here and snuggle with Mommy. Tell me why you're afraid."

"I don't like my new bed. I want to go home."

"Honey, we *are* home. We just stayed in the other place while we were waiting for it to get light again outside. And waiting for it to be warm again, so we could come out of the mine. This will be our home from now on. You'll get used to it, I promise."

The cramped RV in the back of the mine was the only home Markie had ever known.

"No. I don't like it. I'm scared."

"Why don't you like it, honey? What scares you about it?"

"My bed is way too big. It's big enough for monsters to live in. I don't want to wake up and find monsters in my bed. And I can't see you and Daddy from my new bed. I could see you and Daddy before, except when you closed the door. And then I could see the door. But I can't even see your door from my new bed. And I'm scared."

"Oh, honey, I'm so sorry."

She held him close.

"I know for a fact that no monsters will ever get in your bed. No monsters are allowed in this building.

Your daddy put a big sign out in front that says 'Monsters Go Away.' So all of the monsters have to go bother somebody else. They can't even come in here."

"Can't they break in?"

"Nope. We have monster proof locks. We had to order them special from the Monster Proof Store. And your silly daddy, he hung them upside down the first time. So Uncle Bryan had to come and show him how to do it right."

"Daddy *is* pretty silly, huh?"

"You got that right, little buddy. He's sillier than all the sand on the beach."

"No, Mommy. He's sillier than all the stars in the sky."

"No, little sailor. He's sillier than all the water in the ocean."

Markie's face grew serious.

"Mommy?"

"Yes, sir?"

"I've never seen those things… stars and beaches and oceans. Except in picture books. Will I ever get to see them for real?"

She brushed aside some hair that had fallen into eyes.

"Oh, yes. Maybe not the ocean. We're very far away. And the beaches, well, they're the oceans' next door neighbors. We'll try to take you to see both of them someday. But the stars, the stars live right here with us in our new home."

"They do? For the reals?"

"Yes, sir. For the reals."

"When can I see them?"

"I'll tell you what. Tomorrow night we'll ask Daddy how to get up to the roof. And we'll all go up there, and if it's not too cloudy, maybe we can see the stars. Oh, and maybe even the moon too."

His eyes grew as big as saucers.

"The moon too?"

"Yep. If it's out. Sometimes it hides for a few days."

"Oh, I hope it's not hiding. I want to see it *and* the stars."

Hannah turned her head to look at Mark. He was still sleeping like a baby, his mouth open and a long line of drool soaking his pillow. He very softly snored, but not enough to keep anyone else from sleeping.

That, apparently, was little Markie's job.

"Honey, if Mommy lets you snuggle and sleep with her tonight, can we figure out what to do about your bed tomorrow?"

"Okay, deal. And can we put a 'Monsters Go Away' sign on my bedroom door, just in case they accidentally get in?"

"Okay, deal."

He snuggled against Hannah's bosom and put his arm around her. Or at least as far as it would reach. She held him close.

But before she drifted back to sleep, her curiosity got the best of her.

"Markie?"

"Yes, Mommy?"

"How come every time you get scared, you always wake me up instead of your daddy?"

"Because you're softer."

Please enjoy this preview of

THE CLEANSING:

THE CLEANSING

is available now at Barnes and Noble.com and Amazon.com

Ron Bennett was a scumbag. Not in his own eyes, of course. He thought quite highly of himself. As a former President of the United States, he was well known, and people paid him lip service and told him how great he was everywhere he went. But they did that to every former President, simply because, well, how often does the average person ever get a chance to meet one?

So he was fawned over and made to feel special. But nearly everyone really despised him. He hadn't been much of a President, after all. He barely squeaked into office after his predecessor finished a very successful second term and couldn't run again. Bennett, on the other hand, tanked the economy and got the United States into a war with a former soviet bloc country for the worst of reasons. He didn't like the dictator who ran it.

So Bennett did what Presidents sometimes do. He misused his power and had his people develop falsified evidence, false testimony, that this nation was developing weapons capable of destroying Israel and the United States. It was all bullshit. But it's ridiculously easy to deceive a public who doesn't have access to the truth.

It's easy for a crooked politician, whose party controls both houses of congress, to mold the truth into whatever he wants it to be.

So Bennett did that. He sent American troops into a country that had no plans to attack either Israel or the United States. And had they wanted to, they didn't have the means to. What they did have, though, was a strong army which was fiercely loyal to its leader. Loyal enough to die for him. And they did, in vast numbers.

The problem was, they took a lot of Americans along with them. Over 3,000 of them. America's finest. Our sons and daughters. Dead on frozen battlefields half a world away. For nothing. Because Bennett didn't like the man who ran that country.

It wasn't the first time, of course, an American President had started a war for his own ideological reasons. Or to meet his own personal agenda.

It wasn't until Bennett was defeated by a landslide after his first term that rumors started to circulate. And it wasn't until the new President stopped the war and withdrew the American troops from the decimated country that inspectors discovered the extent of the fraud perpetrated on the American people.

UN inspectors discovered no weapons of mass destruction. No nuclear capability. No chemical weapons. No biological weapons. Just millions of rifles, rocket launchers and land mines. Defensive weapons. The kinds of weapons that could be used to ward off a rich, powerful country like the United States for a certain period of time. But not to be a threat to anyone.

And later, Bennett's real motives became known. *American Times Magazine* did an extensive investigation that took two years to complete. They discovered that the whole slew of them- Bennett, his relatives, his friends, friends of friends, all had invested heavily in the defense industry in the months leading up his taking office. Each one of them made tens of millions. So did the friends and families of the Vice President, the Chief of Staff and the Secretary of Defense. But the investments were so well hidden, so well sheltered in blind trusts and overseas reinvestments, that a final accounting was never completed.

And there was nothing illegal about it. That's what outraged Americans most of all. The blood money this group took in exchange for 3,000 American lives broke no rules.

So even though individually they fawned over him, Americans as a group grew to hate this man.

Bennett didn't let that stop him, of course. He did what disgraced politicians always do. He went to ground, stayed on the family ranch for a couple of years, and laid low. He waited for the dust to settle, for the smoke to clear. For people to forget.

Then he very slowly, very carefully, began to reintroduce himself to the public. He became a client of the best public relations firm in the country. They were famous for making the despicable appear tolerable. And they knew their stuff.

They started out by scheduling his appearances at the speaking engagements of other, more popular players. Long-term congressmen who enjoyed approval ratings of over seventy percent in their districts. Senators who were considered up and comers in their political party. Philanthropists who were famous for funding children's hospitals, or shelters for the homeless.

And at some point during each of these events, the cameras would record his presence in the group. Because, after all, he was a former President. And with his permanent detail of four secret service agents, he tended to stick out in a crowd.

And when asked for a comment or interview from a local television station or print reporter, he'd be careful to take the high road.

"Oh, this isn't about me," he'd say. "I'm just here to celebrate the opening of this wonderful new hospital for children's cancer patients."

The goal, of course, was to ease him back into the public spotlight. To make him palatable again. To encourage Americans to forget his transgressions, and bury the past. To let bygones be bygones.

If, a little at a time, he could be seen less and less as a heartless seller of American lives, and more as a misunderstood good guy, then he'd be able to reintegrate into society. Begin sitting on boards of big corporations again. Start rolling in even more and more millions to add to his already vast fortune.

And so it was that he came to be sitting in the audience at Mike Allen's anniversary dinner to celebrate his fortieth year in the United States Senate. He didn't sit at the head table, of course, although they'd offered it to him. He had a table toward the back of the banquet hall, where he could enter without much fanfare and make an early exit if the crowd appeared to be openly hostile toward him.

And it was while sitting at this table, while Allen was in the middle of expressing his gratitude for the people who put on the event, that Ron Bennett's heart exploded. Without warning.

He was dead instantly, of course. As his head fell into his bowl of soup, a secret service agent was on him immediately. Shielding him from further gunshots. A second agent helped him to the floor, where he'd be a harder target. A call went out on a hidden microphone, and the two remaining agents at the exits went on alert, scanning the rafters for threats. Then the crowd.

The first agent had the former President on the floor now, assessing his condition. He quickly determined that the President was dead. He had no respiration or pulse. His face was covered with chicken bisque soup, his eyes wide open.

The agent knew he was dead even before his head slumped. Otherwise his reflexes would have closed his eyes as his head fell forward.

He also quickly realized that Bennett was not felled by a bullet. There was simply no visible wound. He keyed his collar mike and turned his head to the left.

"It looks like natural causes and he's signal 60. Get an ambulance here quickly. No lights, no siren."

The cleansing had begun.

26841971R00140

Made in the USA
Middletown, DE
07 December 2015